# IN HIS DREAMS

OLIVIA PELAR

# Author's Note

This book is intended for audiences 18+ and has the
following trigger warnings:
Murder
Domestic Abuse

# Chapter 1

## Heidi

Casual chatter danced around the room as soft classical music played in the background. Everyone here was dressed better than their usual Sunday's best. Champagne flowed freely as guests celebrated Mountain Wood and Transportation winning their bid for a major contract. Ronny and Duncan's lumber transportation business recently won a contract bid for a local property developer and most of the town was here to congratulate them.

The banquette room at the Lodge had never looked so dressed up. Its bland cream-colored walls were hardly noticeable with all the effort that was put in to transforming the multipurpose room. Hung from the ceiling tiles, a handmade black and gold painted banner read 'Congratulations'. In the far corner of the room, a makeshift bar was set up where beer, wine, and champagne were offered. Carson Bishop and Brendon Leman, two seniors from Mount Hopewell high manned it, ensuring they pointed out their tip jar for their service. Several tables draped with white linin tablecloths dotted the room.

We were all proud of Ronny and Duncan, but all of this felt excessive. So out of character for the residents of Mount Hopewell. We've never celebrated a bid win in the past.

*What makes this one so special?*

That's when I noticed him. Immediately, a wall of tears built behind my eyes, threatening to ruin my mascara if I allowed the dam to break. My eyes were fixed on the man knelt on one knee, holding a black velvet box. An expectant silence swept over the room. Speechless, I reached for my dad standing next to me, and squeezed his arm. He offered me a grin that confirmed my hunch.

Olivia, noticing the halt in chatter, had turned from her conversation with Mrs. Trudy and Mom to find Ronny on one knee, waiting patiently for her attention. Her eyes grew wide and glossy as she used her right hand to cover her mouth. Mom stepped forward and took the glass of champagne from Olivia's left hand. You could hear the smiles from everyone as they moved in closer and surrounded the couple.

Ronny, now reaching for Olivia's left hand, took a steadying breath. "Olivia, we have waited, what feels like an eternity, to start our life together. Throughout these years, you have encouraged me, you've supported me, and most of all, you have loved me. I'm not sure how I became to be so lucky to have someone like you in my corner. To have someone who is so compassionate, and patient, love me is more than I could ever have wished for. I promise that I will spend the rest of my life loving you the way you deserve to be loved. Caring for you the way you deserve to be cared for. And supporting you in all the ways you deserve to be supported. Olivia Rene Miller, will you marry me?"

All eyes shifted to Olivia. A single tear slid down her cheek as she nodded eagerly. "Yes!" she said with a sniffle. "Yes! Of course, I'll marry you!"

The diamond engagement ring that once rested inside the velvet box dazzled on my sister's finger as Ronny slid it into place. The room erupted into celebration as Ronny stood to pull his fiancé in for a kiss, wrapping his arms around her waist and gently lifting her.

The crowd made their way to the newly engaged couple to offer congratulations and hugs. Once the group finally disbursed, Mom, and Mrs. Johnsons rushed around them. Dad, Mr. Johnson, Duncan, and I followed quickly behind them. "Oh, honey, it's just beautiful," Mom sang as she took Olivia's hand to admire her ring.

"Beautiful indeed," Mrs. Johnson agreed as she pulled Olivia in for a hug. "You've been a part of our family for a long time. I'm thrilled that you are one step closer to becoming a Johnson."

"I couldn't agree with you more, hon," Mr. Johnson said as he hugged his son then his future daughter-in-law. "Our Ronny is lucky to have you."

Olivia fanned her face to stop more tears from falling. "I didn't think today would bring tears. Tonight was supposed to be about us congratulating you and Duncan on winning the bid."

"That was just a ploy," Ronny said with a grin for his accomplishment. He wrapped his arm around Olivia's waist and planted a kiss on the top of her head. "I've been planning this for a while."

"It's been a long time coming," Dad said, swallowing back tears of joy. "I cannot imagine a better man to take care of my daughter and I'm thankful that the two of you found each other." Dad then turned and lifted his glass in acknowledgement towards Mr. and Mrs. Johnson. "And I'm thankful that the two of you raised a son that I trust to care for my daughter."

Even though we all knew this day would be here eventually, our emotions were as if Olivia and Ronny's engagement was a total surprise. Drying their eyes with the cocktail napkins they clutched in their hands, Mom and Mrs. Johnson started probing the happy couple with questions about wedding plans.

*I need to get far away from this conversation.*

I was thrilled for my sister, but I worried that the topic would quickly escalate to when *I* planned on settling down. I refused to give my mom the opportunity to ruin my sister's night by turning this into a matrimony hunt.

My mom always stressed how important it is for me to find someone to settle down with, to start my life and plant roots here. Things became especially bad once Olivia and Ronny started dating years ago. My mom almost always found a way to slip in a comment about my lack of a progress towards settling down. More specifically, settling down with Duncan.

Our parents still didn't know that Duncan and I were together, and I didn't plan on telling them any time soon. As soon as my mom found out about us, I was certain she'd try and rush us into a marriage.

My dad asked Duncan if he could accompany him to get another round of champaign for everyone. Duncan gave me an apologetic smile before leaving me here with the already formed wedding brigade. Looking for a way to step away from the conversation unnoticed, Mr. Johnson shot me a look and nodded over his shoulder for me to follow him.

Mr. Johnson was in the beginning of his cancer treatments. He looked frail but he didn't act it. His spirit and personality were still the same high energy, high positivity that had always been there. We walked away from the women unleashing rapid fire questions about wedding colors, themes, and invitations on the unsuspecting couple and found an empty table to sit at. The banquet room was spacious enough to find pockets of quiet, but not large enough to where you felt like you were too far from the action. "So, tell me," Mr. Johnson began, "how is my son doing?"

I thought that was an odd question, seeing how we just left him. But I looked over at Ronny, his face almost matching the shades of pink in his strawberry blonde hair. "I'd say he could use some rescuing from the looks of things. My mom is relentless when it comes to marriage. It's all she cares about…"

Mr. Johnson chuckled and shook his head. "Not Ronny. I'm asking about Duncan. How is Duncan doing?"

Careful not to allude to our relationship, I simply said, "He seems to be doing good. Looks like he and dad are making their way back with the champagne now. Hopefully they're able to make a quick escape after delivering the glasses." Mom had found a pen and started writing only God knows what on a fresh cocktail napkin. Wedding planning was in full swing whether Olivia and Ronny were ready or not.

"Heidi," Mr. Johnson said, pulling my attention away from the chaos that ensued. "Your secret is safe with me. Although, I don't understand why the two of you would want to keep it a secret. You and Duncan may not be able to recognize it, but I certainly can. Everyone can. The two of you, together, it's something real. Something that not everyone is lucky to have."

I tucked my hair behind my ear and looked down at my hands unsure of what to say or do. We weren't ready to let anyone else in on our secret. I looked back to Mr. Johnson, his eyes glinted with knowledge. I didn't want to lie to him, but Duncan and I were figuring things out. Not wanting our parents to influence us, we agreed not to tell them yet.

"It's alright. You don't have to tell me. But can you make me a promise?" Mr. Johnsons asked when I had no other words to offer. "Will you keep an eye on him? He has overcome terrible circumstances to have grown into the strong and capable man that he is today. I know his exterior seems tough, but inside, I worry that he's still harboring the boy we brought home all those years ago." Mr. Johnson's eyes shifted from me to something behind me, "A young boy shouldn't have to waste years of his childhood trying to heal."

"Heal from what?" I blurted out. I knew Ducan had an upsetting childhood before the Johnsons adopted him, but no one knew why. It's the only secret in Mount Hopewell. Curiosity had always been there, but I'd never pushed to find out.

Mr. Johnson shook his head regretfully. "I'm sorry, but it's not my story to tell."

"I understand." I shook the tendril loose with my nod before tucking it back behind my ear.

"But," he started with his sanguine tone, "whatever you did to help him through the acceptance of my diagnosis seemed to be just what the doctor ordered. So, keep up the good work!" He branded a silly smile and thumbs up.

A nervous laugh slipped through my lips involuntarily. I'm not so sure he would want me to keep up the good work if he knew what I did to help Duncan. Goosebumps rolled across my skin at the memory.

About a week ago, Mr. Johnson told his family that he was diagnosed with stage three stomach cancer. He had known about his diagnosis for a while but only decided to tell his family once he was accepted as a candidate for a clinical trial. The clinical trial hoped to have his cancer in remission within the next 18 months. It was aggressive, but he and his doctors are optimistic. Mrs. Johnson and Ronny were understandably devastated, but Duncan retreated to somewhere inside himself. Somewhere he hadn't been since he was a kid, according to Ronny. Both times, once as a child, then again after being told about his dad's diagnosis, Duncan rendered himself speechless. Ronny and Mr. Johnson thought I'd be the only one to help him overcome whatever it was he was hiding from. At the time, I was positive I wasn't what Duncan needed, but he proved otherwise.

"I didn't think we'd ever get out of there," Dad said as he and Duncan approached the table. Motioning towards the wedding planning mothers, he continued as he took his seat. "They tried to rope us into a conversation about centerpieces."

Duncan offered me a new glass of champagne. Our eyes locked as his fingers lingered on mine. His green eyes danced over the length of my neck.

Electricity ran through my fingers and straight to my nipples, causing me to swallow hard. "Thanks," I said breathlessly.

The sharp, repeated clinks from Mr. Johnson tapping his fork against his glass demanded everyone's attention. "Speech!" he yelled, distracting me from my lustful thoughts.

# Chapter 2

## Duncan

As my older brother stood in front of his guests earlier in the evening, gushing over his fiancé and thanking everyone for coming out, all I could focus on was her.

Ronny asked that everyone come dressed as extravagant as their closets would allow, and Heidi didn't disappoint. The black dress she wore clung to her body. Two long sleeves split by a plunging neckline that teased at the vision underneath. The length of her dress was just enough to cover her wide hips and ass. Had she not been wearing black tights to protect her lower half from the evening chill, one wrong move would have exposed everything. My cock ached for her. My fingertips twitched with restraint from touching her. Even the line of her neck taunted me, begging to be kissed.

Heidi Miller made me feel things I didn't yet understand. This was more than an attraction. Instead, it felt more like a binding. After all these years, I was finally tired of fighting it.

My boots landed heavily on the stairs of Heidi's back porch as I took two at a time to reach her back door in record time. The door flew opened before I could knock. I swept her up in my arms as I crossed the threshold and kicked the door closed behind me. She crashed into my body with force as she wrapped her arms and bare legs around me, pressing her warm sex against my stomach. Her hands slid into the shoulders of my jacket, helping me shake out of the sleeves one arm at a time. Her lips were hungry for mine as our tongues swirled and flicked together. Warmth rushed to the head of my cock as my lips moved to her neck. Kisses trailed from under her chin to the top of her shoulder where the ban…

"Heidi," I said abruptly and breathy, forgetting to be gentle with her. The gold hues in her hazel eyes darkened like honey as she stared at me with frustration. "You're still healing. We should take it easy."

She rolled her eyes, "It's a superficial wound. Those scissors barely made a mark."

It had only been five days since she was stabbed. I saw the wound, it left more than *barely* a mark. It wasn't a deep gash thankfully, but she'll have a scar from it.

"A couple of those little strips fixed me right up," she said as the gold returned to her eyes.

"Butterfly bandages are not a cure-all." Her charm didn't dissipate my worry. "You're still not supposed to be moving your shoulder aggressively."

"Fine." She kissed my lips. "I'll take it slow. " She kissed my neck once. Twice. Three times before I realized I had taken us to her room, her legs still wrapped around me.

She slid down my body to stand in front of me. Her eyes locked with mine as she began to loosen my tie. I wrapped my hand around hers to stop her. "Lay down," I instructed, nodding my head in the direction of the bed.

With an alluring grin, she found her place as I

removed my tie and unbuttoned the first two buttons of my shirt. Heidi watched me curiously as I leaned forward, my hands moving slowly up her legs. Goosebumps followed in the wake of my fingers as they traveled higher up to her thighs.

She was beautiful.

The way she watched me watching her. The way her body reacted to mine. All of it was more than I was worth. I didn't understand why she wanted to be with me, but I was grateful that she was. And I needed her to know.

I knelt in front of her bed, grabbed the outside of her bare thighs, then carefully pulled her body closer towards me. The hem of her dress rolled up over her hips, exposing the black cotton panties she wore underneath. I dragged the tip of my nose up then down her slit, reveling in the gasp I coaxed from her. My fingers traced the hems of her panties before finally hoking them at her sides and pulling them down, uncovering her sex. Spreading Heidi's legs wider, I pulled her completely to the edge of the bed. Leaning forward, I landed a single kiss at the top of her mound, rewarding me with another gasp.

My hands found their way to her hips and held her in place. Like a missile searching for its target, my tongue greedily sought the wetness between her folds. Heidi tried to buck her hips in response, but I held her firmly, determined to take things *slow*. She continued to squirm against my face as my lips sucked and my tongue danced around her clit. With every few tugs of her clit, I slid my tongue in and out of her opening, making my dick jealous. Her hands gripped the sheets beneath her as she groaned softly.

Heidi's hips tilted upward slightly, and I knew she was close. I could feel her body straining against the hold of my grip. Her hands found my hair, "Duncan," she whimpered, still trying to buck harder against my face. "Please."

Loosening my grip on her, her hips moved freely as my tongue continued its dance up and down her. Her hips, tilting higher still, I inserted two fingers, coaxing her release until I felt her insides quiver. Finally, I could feel the slickness against my mouth and fingers as her moans filled my ears. I closed my eyes, allowing her undoing to overtake all my senses. My erection pushed uncomfortably against the zipper of my slacks. I would have to relieve myself later.

Finding the panties I removed from her earlier, I dried my mouth and beard with them then tossed them in the hamper.

Heidi lifted herself up on her strong arm while pushing the hem of her dress back down over her hips. "Your turn," she said hungrily eying my bulge. The thought almost made me trip over my own feet. What I wouldn't give to feel her hot mouth around me, but it would have to wait. I wanted tonight to just be about her. Before I could answer, she was up and on her way to the bathroom. "Shower with me?"

As difficult as it was to say no to sharing a hot, steamy shower where our wet naked bodies would brush against each other, I needed to get home before I had a permanent imprint of a zipper down my shaft. If I were to go in there with her, she would find a way to wear me down and take matters into her own hands. Literally. And her shoulder still needed to heal. "How about a rain check? I need to stop by the

Lodge and make sure nothing was left behind from tonight."

Heidi pouted, tempting me with her lips. "Fine." Her hands reached behind her and pulled at the zipper of her dress. Sliding the sleeves off her arms, the fabric fell at her feet. "I'll be waiting for you to get back," she turned and sauntered away.

***

Before I stopped by the Lodge, I headed to my house for a shower and some relief. The swelling in my dick had barely subsided by the time I arrived home. Once the shower had reached a comfortable temperature, I stood under its stream, with my hand wrapped around my shaft. Heidi's naked body was on full display in my mind. And the way her bottom lip stuck out, beckoning the head of my penis, had me close to unraveling already. It didn't take many strokes down my length before my load escaped, pulling my muscles tight to allow the ecstasy to roll through me. With a grunt, I pressed the palm of my free hand against the wall for support. *Heidi.*

She was it for me and somewhere inside, I had always known that. Working through my issues steadily but slowly, was no longer a choice I could afford. If I wanted to be the man that Heidi deserved, I needed to find myself. Confront the past that had held me prisoner within my own mind since I was a child. If I could only remember what happened, I could move on from it.

I feared if I never figured it out, my mind would always wander back to it, never allowing me to fully focus on my present, or my future with Heidi.

In the past, whenever I'd asked my parents what happened before they adopted me, they always respond the same way – they weren't sure what happened. All they were told was that a child had suffered memory loss, possible selective mutism, and was in need of a family. The agency they adopted me from didn't have any additional details to share with them.

They said I didn't speak for two years after arriving in Mount Hopewell. At the time, they weren't sure if I couldn't talk or simply wouldn't. I don't remember much of that time, but I do recall having to meet with a child therapist often. As my parents reminded me, the diagnosis was traumatic mutism. From what trauma, I couldn't remember.

That's what had been eating at me all this time. How could I forget something that inflicted such a response? Why couldn't I remember my family from before? How come no one ever claimed me?

According to the therapist I secretly started to see shortly after my brother and I got the business up and running, all of these questions resulted in insecurities that I was unable to overcome. Insecurities that allowed me to lose Heidi once before. I didn't want to fuck up and lose her again.

In this past week alone, I have endured the fear of losing her for good on two separate occasions. The first was when she never returned home after leaving with that shrink, Dr. Keller. She was asleep, stuck in a dream, for three days, and none of the nurses or the doctor could figure out why.

Heidi had recently learned of her ability to

Connect. As she explained it, Connecting was when two people were able to seek out and connect with each other's dreams. This was originally only thought to be possible when both individuals were in an R.E.M cycle at the same time. What she had later learned was that the other individual didn't have to be experiencing a R.E.M cycle at all. She could Connect to any unconscious energy. An unconscious energy from dreamers, passed out hikers, and coma patients to name a few.

It was theorized that the reason she was asleep for three days was because she was Connecting with a coma patient – which happened to be the doctor's husband, Martin Keller. Once she did finally wake up from her unintentional, three-day long nap, she ran directly toward a more tangible threat, making my fear nearly a reality a second time.

That night in the basement of Keller Institute could have ended the both of us. During that three-day Connection with the Martin, Heidi had learned some incriminating details that implicated the doctor of her involvement of trying to murder him. With the way we rushed back to the institute, Dr. Keller assumed that we knew the truth of how he wound up in that coma. Her son, Graham, confronted her first. Heidi and noticed Dr. Keller's hand lift, prepared to take a strike when she rushed forward and pushed Graham out of the way. The mad woman was wielding a pair of scissors. If the blow had landed any higher on her shoulder, closer to her neck, Heidi would have likely died from her wound. Fortunately, it appeared that Dr. Keller didn't possess enough physical strength to inflict any detrimental damage.

Instead, Heidi sported a superficial wound on her left shoulder.

She said she felt fine, and it was no longer bothering her like it had been a few days prior, but I still worried.

Not only did I worry about her wound, but I also worried that I may not be the only man on her mind. Her ability to Connect was shared with Graham. The two of them were in that three-day Connection together. When I finally learned of where she was, I of course rushed to her. When I found her though, she was lying in his bed, beside him, each of them wearing a cap full of wires that lead to a few machines. Seeing her laying there with another man did something to me that I didn't like.

It wasn't like we hadn't both dated other people in the past, but neither of us flaunted it. Not that it ever lasted long enough to flaunt, but still, I had never felt what I felt then.

Foolish, stupid even, for breaking her heart all those years ago.

# Chapter 3

## Heidi

*The gray walls that once frightened me now only reminded me of all that he lost. Yet, there he stood, trying to right his mother's wrongs and continue her work in the way it should have been intended – to help others. The gray room of the basement at the Keller Institute was where I knew I could always find Graham.*

*"So, what do you think?" I sat nervously under his pensive stare, awaiting his response. If he agreed, it could mean everything. A job, a life, a love that I had always dreamed of. And I could do it all from Mount Hopewell.*

*I had decided that I no longer wanted to move to the city. What I wanted was to remain home and continue running the store with my sister. And by night, I wanted to help patients through Connections.*

*"If that is the only way for you to be involved with the institute, then I think it's a great idea."*

*I squealed with excitement and shot to my feet. "So, when can I start?"*

*"You can start now if you want. I have a patient that keeps talking about the woman who helped him clean his apartment."*

*"Eric?" Graham nodded and confirmed. "How is he? He didn't seem to be doing too well when I saw him last. I haven't tried to Connect with him since everything happened."*

"He wants to get better. And he's putting in the effort. But he's struggling."

Eric and I met, unofficially, in a dream. He was a recovering alcoholic who had trouble obtaining sobriety from rehabs and Alcohol Anonymous programs in the past. He talked as if the Keller Institute was his last hope of recovery and finding a spot in his daughter's life. "How can I help?"

"We've been trying to work with him on confronting his alcoholism by putting himself in a triggering environment and denying his urge to drink. But at each session, he reports that he doesn't deny himself the drink. He's been avoiding alcohol during the day, but I can tell he's wavering. If he's going to overcome his addiction, he has to find the strength to say 'No'."

"Alright, I'll look for him." I took a cleansing breath ready to search for Eric, but Graham called my attention.

"Before you go… how are things?"

I've only interacted with Graham on one other occasion and that was last night. He Connected with me to ask if I had made a decision about working at the Keller Institute yet. I told him I needed a little more time. I then quickly put myself somewhere else, away from his Connection, in case he tried to influence my decision in anyway. This was a choice I needed to make on my own.

Still, I should have made more of an effort to check in on him. He lost his mom then his dad in the same night. I'm sure that wasn't easy to deal with alone. "Things have been good. My sister and her boyfriend are finally engaged. My shoulder is feeling better every day. And now I get the opportunity to have a job that matters." I left out the fact that I was deliriously happy that Duncan and I were together. I wasn't sure how long it would last, or if I would wind up getting my heart broken again.

"That's good. I'm glad things are going well. I wanted to tell you, the apartment below mine is available if you change your mind and decide to move to the city."

"Oh sure, I'll move in there with all the money I have saved up," I scoffed jokingly.

"It's already taken care of. All you have to do is say the word and it's yours."

"What..."

Behind him, a bright green light flashed against the gray walls. Shielding my eyes with my arm, I squinted and watched green and yellow hues dance in unison, rippling across the ceiling.

"Does that mean anything to you?" he asked, referring to the show of lights.

The last time I saw lights like these in a dream, they lead me to Duncan, just as I sensed they would. The tightening in my chest and tingling on my neck told me they would lead me to him again. Without saying a word to Graham, I had already started moving towards the lights.

The greens and yellows were quickly replaced with white. White beneath me, white above me. Snow blanketed the ground below and clung to the bare tree branches above. Illuminated by the moonlight just ahead, sat a small house. Its exterior appeared to be in shambles. I squinted my eyes for a better look and suddenly I was standing directly in front of the *house. The cement steps leading up to the front porch were crumbling. Fine lines ripped through the faded blue paint. The door hung haphazardly from its top hinge. My feet and ankles began to feel numb. But I looked onward, ignoring the pain growing from the tips of my toes. Just inside the doorway, a puddle of darkness pooled.*

What was that?

*"Heidi!" A concerned voice sounded from behind me.*

*Graham hurried toward me with challenged steps, his feet getting buried in pillows of snow with each movement. I suddenly realized the chilling tingles from the snow had spread beyond the tips of my toes. My teeth clattered uncontrollably in response to the cold. He wrapped his arms around me and rubbed my back. The friction worked hard to warm me up. I buried my head in his chest seeking more warmth.*

*A creak from inside the house echoed out from the doorway.*

*"Stop!" A small voice yelled from inside the house.*

*"Someone's in there!" I cried, pushing away from Graham towards the collapsing cement steps.*

*His arms tightened around me, "Heidi, no one is in there."*

*"Stop! Get away from her!" The voice called again.*

*"Yes there is!" I pushed against him again and finally broke free of his grip, landing on my hands and knees. The snow bit aggressively at my bare palms.*

*A tall shadow slithered across the doorway. The*

*thud of heavy footsteps with rhythmic clinking caused my heart to race with nervousness and realization. There was something familiar about this place.*

This was not the first time I had been here.

***

Sitting at my kitchen table the following morning, I replayed the events of my dream over and over in my mind. The first question I tried to answer was why did the green and yellow lights lead me somewhere unexpected? I was certain they would lead me to Duncan, but they hadn't. Identifying markers in a Connection was like giving someone a name. It was how I could identify a familiar Connection. But this time, the lights hadn't led me to Duncan and I wondered if they were maybe a marker for someone else instead.

The house though, the house I had seen before. The question I struggled with was, had I seen that house in a dream before, or had I actually been there once?

After mulling it over for a moment, I decided that I couldn't have seen the house in person before. Reminding myself of my lack of adventurous traveling, I was certain I had not seen this house firsthand before. However, if I had dreamed it, why couldn't I remember how it ended?

The sputtering from the coffee maker turned to a hiss, temporarily halting the ricocheting questions that flew around my mind. I retrieved two coffee cups from the cabinet and sat them near the coffee pot. I filled one nearly to the brim and left room for milk in the other, before taking my mug back to my seat.

I blew on the surface of my coffee as Duncan made his way to the kitchen, wearing nothing but light gray sweatpants. The outline of his girth teased the fabric that concealed it.

I hadn't been able to stay up and wait for him last night. By the time he got back, I had already dozed off, only slightly stirring once he climbed into bed with me and pulled me close.

"Good morning," he said with his sexy, gravely morning voice. He jaunted towards me, placing a kiss on the top of my head, and instantly causing a smile to awaken on my lips.

"Morning," I said warmly. "Coffee is on the counter for you. Made just the way you like it – with enough room for you to make it gross."

"Adding milk to coffee is an acceptable way to drink it," he said with a chuckle. "You might like it if you'd try it." Shutting the door to the fridge, gallon in hand as he approached the counter where his mug sat, I watched as he poured milk in his perfectly good coffee, diluting the life force that we would inevitably need.

My mom and Mrs. Johnson called everyone together this morning. We're meeting everyone over at Ronny's house to discuss wedding plans. Olivia and Ronny hadn't been engaged for twenty-four hours yet and my mom had already gone into full blown planning mode. When I asked who was going to care for the store during this, she causally mentioned that everyone already knew it'd be closed today. Apparently she alerted everyone last night at the party but didn't inform any of us until this morning. "No thanks. I will need all the caffeine I can get before making an appearance." Lifting my mug to my mouth, I closed my eyes as I took a sip, letting the warmth spread through me.

"It can't be that bad," he said naively, taking his seat next to me.

"You're in for a treat." I scoffed, blowing on my coffee, attempting to keep the surfaced cooled down. "Marriage is my mom's main goal for Olivia and me. It's all she wants for us. To get married, start a family, raise our kids here, and keep the store running. It's like, if we don't, she has somehow failed as a mother. It feels like marriage is how she measures our 'success' as adults." Rolling my eyes at my mom's frustrating standards for us, I took a scorching gulp from my mug and slouched in my chair, already worn from the day ahead. "You should probably get back to your house soon so you can get ready. And before too many people have the opportunity to see you leaving from the trail head." We needed to be more cautious at hiding our relationship. I didn't want anyone to find out that we were together.

Duncan looked down at his mug full of fresh coffee with a splash of bad decision, "Oh, uh, yeah. Right." He stared pensively at his coffee.

"You can take the coffee to go, of course."

"Okay," he nodded stiffly. "Thanks." Duncan excused himself from the table and disappeared around the corner. A few moments later, he returned wearing different clothes and had a small black duffle bag in hand. "I'll see you later," he said as he bent down to kiss the top of my head again. He picked up his coffee and raised it to me on the way out the back door. "Thanks again."

I took a deep breath in and exhaled. "Let's get this over with," I said to myself. Looking for my phone, I texted Olivia that I'd be there in twenty.

Pulling up to Ronny's, I noticed I was the last one to arrive. I entered his house without knocking and followed the sounds of chatter to the dining room. "Good morning, sweetheart," Dad said as he noticed my arrival.

"Morning, Dad." I made my way toward him where he sat around the table and placed a kiss on his cheek. In addition to my dad, Ronny, Olivia, and Mr. Johnson were all sitting around it, each with steaming mugs of coffee. But no sign of Duncan.

"Good morning, honey," Mom called from the kitchen as she heard the exchange between me and Dad.

Mom and Mrs. Jonson stood with their backs to me as I entered the kitchen. Mrs. Johnson was busy cooking something on the stove while my mom manned the griddle full of pancakes. I approached the kitchen island, rested my palms on the ledge, and leaned in slightly as I took in the breakfast spread the two of them prepared. "Morning, Mama." Her hands flipped the last pancake on the griddle before turning to blow me a quick air kiss.

"Good morning, Mrs. Johnson."

"Good morning, Heidi," she said while keeping her eye on the stove. "Hope you're hungry."

"I definitely am." My stomach growled from the delicious smells that swirled around me. "Is there anything I could help with?"

"Sure. Could you grab the plates and start setting the table? Then we can start bringing the food out."

Familiar footfalls sounded behind me. "I can give you a hand with that," Duncan said. Approaching the kitchen island where I stood, his hand softly grazed my lower back as he passed me. I wasn't sure if it was intentional or not, but electricity had sparked across my skin from his fingers. I stepped away from him quickly and grabbed the heavy stoneware plates.

"Let me grab those." He effortlessly claimed the stack of stoneware from my hands.

"Thanks." I noticed something in his eyes, something he was trying to hide. I cleared my throat, reminding myself of where I was and that the middle of his brother's kitchen wouldn't be the best place to ask him about it. "I'll bring the napkins and silverware," I said, to replace the words I wanted to speak.

Folling Duncan to the dining room, he made himself busy by placing the plates in front of each seat. I followed suit, placing the silverware and a napkin next to each plate. Mom and Mrs. Johnson entered the dining room with dishes of food. Eggs, pancakes, and French toast, followed by bacon, sausage, biscuits, and gravy filled the center of the table.

Taking my seat across the table from Duncan, I readied myself for uncomfortable conversations and invasive questions. Thankfully, the chatter flowed easily between everyone as we all enjoyed our breakfast. Afterwards, the men cleared the table of dirty dishes so we could move to the next phase of this gathering – planning a long-awaited wedding.

"I'll be right back," Olivia said as she excused herself from the table quickly. She returned with a tiny white gift bag and set it on the table in front of me. "Here. This is for you." Her hands folded behind her back, and she wore a giddy grin.

"Me?" I felt my eyebrow arch curiously at her. "You're the one who's newly engaged. Shouldn't I be getting something for you?"

"There's still time," she joked. "Just opened it."

The first thing I pulled out was a handwritten note that read:

*Heidi,*
*Will you be my…*

I reached into the bag and pulled out a wad of yellow tissue paper. It felt so light that if the windows were opened, a gentle breeze would blow it right out of my hand. I carefully unwrapped the paper to reveal its contents. Underneath sat a friendship bracelet. One that was similar in style to the ones we made as kids. The thread was rainbow colored with letter beads that spelled out…*maid of honor*. Nostalgia caused my lips to curve into a smile. "Of course!" I sprang from my seat to pull her into a hug. "When did you have time to make this?"

"When I was twelve."

"Huh?"

"I made that bracelet when we were kids. Remember how sometimes we'd dress up for our M.A.S.H weddings?" I nodded. Memories of us walking around on our tippy toes, wearing mom's night gowns as make-believe wedding dresses flooded my mind. "I made this for you to wear then, but decided I wanted to give it to you when it was for real." She then reached into the back pocket of her jeans and pulled out a matching bracelet. Instead, the letter beads on hers spelled 'Bride'.

Tears threatened my eyes "I can't believe you've kept up with these all these years." I noticed Olivia's eyes were glassy too. I pulled her into another hug in hopes that it would stop both of our tears. I'd never understand how I got so lucky to have a sister as wonderful as her.

"Oh no. What happened?" Ronny asked concerned, rounding the corner of the dining room.

"Olivia asked Heidi to be her maid of honor with bracelets she made when they were kids," Mom sniffled.

"How did you ask Duncan to be your Best Man?" Mrs. Johnson asked her son.

Ronny looked at Duncan who had appeared next to him, then to his mom, "I'm supposed to ask him?"

"Yes," we all said in unison. Causing Ronny to flinch playfully at our response.

"Ask me what?" Duncan inquired as he returned.

He turned to Duncan, "You want to be my Best Man?"

"Yeah, why not," Duncan shrugged. They leaned in for a hug that ended with a quick slap on the back.

"Boys," Mrs. Johnson said with amusement, turning her back to them and facing us women again.

Everyone else took their seats back at the table. Mom pulled out a notepad and pen, "Alright, let's get started. Have the two of you picked a date yet?"

# Chapter 4

## Heidi

The wedding planning breakfast turned into the wedding planning lunch. I was sure an entire wedding had never been planned with such a quickness before. But I guessed that's what happens when Maxine Miller was the one who led the planning. The only other thing that needed to be decided was the date. Olivia has had her heart set on a certain style of dress, and she wanted to make sure she could find exactly what she wanted before they settled on a date.

Duncan was the first to leave this afternoon, followed by our parents shortly after. I waited for them to be good and gone before I said my goodbyes to Ronny and Olivia and headed to Duncan's house.

Ronny and Olivia were the first people we told, and I hated to admit it, but it was a relief when Duncan and I didn't have to pretend not to be in a relationship. It was hard to keep up the appearance of just "friends".

But, I wondered what it'd be like to not have to keep up the charade. My mom didn't make a single remark about marriage to me today. No accusing tones, no inappropriate questions about my dating life or when I planned to settle down. It wasn't like her at all. *Maybe she was coming down with something.*

My thoughts, like laundry in a dryer, doubts, concerns, and hopes all tumbled around my head quickly. What if we *did* tell our parents, and it ultimately didn't work out between us? Then, regardless of whose fault it may be, my mom would undoubtedly blame me for it.

What if he didn't feel for me, the way I felt for him? He said he could see us settling down together, but that was when he thought I was moving to the city. What if he said all those sweet things because he wouldn't have to follow through with action. *No. Duncan is a man of his word. He's honest and good.*

The conflicting thoughts painfully ping ponged around my brain the rest of the drive to Duncan's house, making me nauseous in the short drive.

My relationship with Duncan shouldn't have been in the forefront of my mind when I had bigger issues to address. I didn't Connect with Eric last night, even though I knew he needed me. I followed the lights that appeared instead, thinking it would lead me to Duncan. But when it led me to the battered house, I spent a lot of my morning trying to remember the original dream, not focusing on Eric like I should have.

If I wanted to get the guy *and* the job, I'd have to start making them both an equal priority in my life. Pulling into Duncan's driveway, I decided that I would focus on patient Connections first, then I could explore others when needed. But for now, I was looking forward to spending quality time with the handsome man inside.

"I think that went really well." Duncan said as I settled next to him on the couch. "I only understood a third of what you all were talking about, but everyone seemed to be happy with all the decisions made today."

"It did go well, didn't it?" Surprisingly, I agreed. "Olivia's face was glowing with excitement when we left. And my mom didn't fuss about my dating life once. I think that's the first time in my adult life that I've been in a room with her that didn't end with us having an argument." Duncan's expression changed to a half smile and a raised eyebrow, as if I was exaggerating. "I'm serious," I said with a laugh. "She is truly relentless. If we're not arguing about when I plan on settling down, we're arguing about my dreams."

Duncan tucked my hair behind my ear before wrapping his arm around me and pulling me closer to his warm body. "How have your dreams been lately?"

I thought about last night's dream. What did Graham mean when he said it was taken care of if I wanted the apartment below him? How could I have ignored Eric when I knew he needed me? Why couldn't I remember the ending of the house dream?

"They've been…thought provoking." I looked up at him and wrapped my arm around his wide torso, "I think I had a reoccurring dream, or part of a reoccurring dream last night. But if it was, I haven't been able to remember how it's supposed to end. It's been rattling around in the back of my head all day. Oh! And I forgot to tell you – Graham is on board! I will live here, still run the store with Olivia, and assist patients while I dream."

Duncan endured my ramblings with nods and a smile, "That's amazing, babe." He dipped his head down and used his free hand to gently tilt my chin upwards to meet his kiss.

"Thank you," I said with a proud grin. "Now all

that's left to do is decide if I should tell my parents or not." It was a rhetorical question. Of course, I should tell them. The question really was *how* I was going to tell them. I could feel Duncan's chest expand slightly, ready to respond with reason but mentally, I had already moved on. "How's your dad doing? He seemed as well as he could be last night."

Duncan expelled the breath he held in his chest. "He says he's feeling good. And for the most part, he seems like his dependably happy self. We're taking it as a positive sign that this clinical trial will be successful. But it has got me thinking…" He sat facing me, with one knee on the couch, his arm thrown over the back of it. "I think we should tell our parents."

The air between us went thin. I was silent. Stunned. Part of me felt relieved, part of me felt terrified.

"I don't want to have to hide us anymore. I barely restrained myself from wrapping my arm around your waist this morning at breakfast."

My head nodded slightly, trying to slow my thoughts. I nervously twisted the rainbow-colored thread bracelet that now took up space on my right wrist. "Yeah. I don't want to hide us anymore either." My heart raced with excitement and nervousness simultaneously. "Duncan," I said with a shaky breath. He stared expectantly at me, waiting for my words. Fear entangled its roots deeper in my belly.

The last time we did this, things did not go as I expected. And I was terrified I would suffer the same outcome this time. But if we were going to do this, I needed to put it all on the table. I needed him to know.

With a final calming breath, I released the words I held close to my chest for the past ten years. "I love you."

Duncan's green eyes brightened, and his pupils grew a fraction wider. His grin landed on me, making me lightheaded with a buzz. His hands cupped the sides of my face, his thumb stroked my cheek. "Heidi, I love you, too."

I let out the breath I didn't know I had been holding with my smile. *Duncan Johnson loves me back.*

I leaped into his lap, wrapping my arms around his neck, and began kissing him deeply. His hands found their way to my backside, gripping the sides of my ass, pulling me in closer to his groin. I felt him thickening beneath my greedy sex.

Definitely not the reaction I expected, but the one I had hoped for.

Our hands, tongues, and breath came to an abrupt halt when we heard gravel crunch outside. We paused, holding our bodies completely still until we heard the slam of two car doors.

I swore under my breath, irritated by the interruption. I scurried off Duncan's lap and tried to sit causally next to him as footsteps sounded up the front porch steps. Ronny landed a quick knock before letting Olivia then himself inside.

"Hey," Olivia said as her curious gaze swept from Duncan then to me, "Hope we're not interrupting anything, but I wanted to return this." She and Ronny took a seat on the love seat next to us. She placed a yellow mug that read 'Best Little Sister Ever' in orange font on the coffee table between us. It was the same cup I poured Duncan's coffee into this morning. The mug was part of a set that our parents got us one year for Christmas. Olivia had the other that said, 'Best Big Sister Ever'.

"I saw it sitting on the kitchen island this morning when Mom asked if I would put on a fresh pot of coffee. I felt bad since the coffee was still warm, but I emptied it out then stashed it in the dish washer to hide it from her and Dad. Didn't want your cover to be blown by a mug."

"You think they would have been found out by a cup?" Ronnie asked.

"Maybe not by your parent's, but by ours? Definitely. Especially since they were the ones to gift me and Heidi the mugs."

Ronny and Duncan shared a confused look. It seemed they didn't quite understand how something so inconspicuous could be such a threat.

Deciding to help them out, I informed them that, "It would have definitely raised suspicion between the parents had any of them noticed a "little sister" mug at Ronny's house when I wasn't there." The guy's confused expressions shifted to understanding. That seemed to do it, they were following along now. Although, I wondered why Duncan brought the mug with him to their house. And the coffee was still hot. Didn't he have to go home to get ready?

Then I remembered the duffle bag he had when he left.

That was when I noticed he was wearing the same clothes he put on this morning before he left my house. Had he intended for us to show up to breakfast together?

# Chapter 5

## Duncan

"You really are the most amazing sister," Heidi beamed at Olivia.

"I know," Olivia replied jokingly. "Well, we'll get going. We're running over to Mom and Dad's. Dad left his readers. He probably hasn't even noticed they're missing yet," she chuckled.

Since this morning hadn't gone as planned, and with the support of my brother already behind me, I figured now was as good a time as any. "We could take those."

"We?" Heidi questioned.

I took her hand and nodded. I wanted this. I wanted her. I wanted *us*. I was a fool to walk away from her before.

I could see the thoughts running through that beautifully complicated mind of hers. After a moment, she nodded too, sending my heart into a rhythmic dance of elation.

Ronny and Olivia wore matching expressions, "Well, it's about damn time, man." Ronny said.

"It sure is!" Olivia echoed Ronny's sentiment. "I was surprised to see you arrive alone this morning."

"What do you mean?" Heidi asked, her eyes darted between me and her sister. "Were we *supposed* to come together?"

"I had planned to talk to you about it this morning since you had already fallen asleep once I got back last night. That's why I brough my bag. But you seemed to have had a lot on your mind and I wasn't sure if I should bring it up or not." Heidi's face fell, her confused expression turned flat. Once again, I saw the thoughts unleash themselves within her mind.

"So," Heidi's eyes darted to Olivia, "you were okay with us showing up together, on the morning we were set to plan your wedding, to let everyone know that Duncan and I were dating?"

"Yes! We don't want the two of you sneaking around, hiding your relationship, any more than you do."

There had been so much going on, personally, in each of our lives, I wasn't sure when the right time would be to tell everyone. But almost immediately, Olivia and Ronny both had been advocates for us to come clean to our parents. And the rest of the town for that matter.

Heidi nodded, like she was considering her next words carefully. "So, we're going to tell them. Now?" Her eyes drifted back to mine, looking for an answer.

"Only if you want."

After a few moments, Heidi's eyes softened, and her posture straightened. "I do. Let's tell them."

Olivia clasped her hands together, bringing them over her heart. "Can we come?!" Olivia asked, nearly falling out of her seat with excitement. "I'm dying to see Mom's reaction."

"Oh man. Mom is going to lose it, isn't she?"

"Yes," the couple said in unison.

Heidi stood and took a deep breath, "Well, let's get this over with before I chicken out."

The four of us loaded up into our respective cars

and headed down the road to my parent's house. Their car wasn't in the driveway, so we headed to the Millers instead. As it turned out, my parents were there too. At least this way, we will be able to tell them all at the same time.

Olivia and Ronny entered the Millers' house first, followed by me and Heidi. "Hi, kids. Long time no see," Arnold joked from his recliner "What brings you all by?"

Mom and Maxine came shuffling down the hallway as they heard the commotion.

Olivia approached her dad, "You forgot these over at Ronny's."

"Well, that was mighty nice of the *four* of you to bring me my glasses," Arnold said with a suspicious smile.

"Is everything alright?" Mom asked after an awkward silence filled the cramped living room.

I led Heidi to the couch where we both took a seat. Olivia and Ronny stood behind us. "Yes, everything is fine, Mom. But we'd like to discuss something with you all." The words were desperate to leave my lips. They had been daring to escape since the party last night.

"No," Heidi said suddenly, halting my confession.

My heart sopped. I could hear Olivia suck in a sharp breath behind us.

"We're not here to *discuss* anything," Heidi shot me a reassuring glance. "We're here to *tell* you," she corrected.

Before my smile could fully crest, I took her hand in mine. A notion the parents didn't miss. "Heidi and I are together." I felt Heidi's hand flinch slightly under mine. Before the words had a chance to settle in everyone's ears, Maxine's eyes grew wide.

"Oh! I knew it! I just knew it!" Maxine sang. She rushed over to us where she squeezed Heidi's cheeks and kissed her on her forehead then did the same to me. "This is wonderful news! My oldest is getting married and now my youngest is making an effort in her life to be happy."

Heidi's hand went molten in mine. I was sure she was reacting to her mom's choice of words. I gently squeezed her hand to remind her she wasn't alone. From the corner of my eye, I saw Olivia place her hand on Heidi's shoulder, likely reminding her of the same. A soft breath left Heidi's lips and I felt her relax.

It was Mom's turn to congratulate us. She and Maxine sat on the couch opposite of us. "So, when did this happen?" she asked excitedly.

"About a week ago."

"I think I speak for all of us here when I say we're thrilled that the two of you have finally come to your senses," Dad laughed.

"Agreed," Arnold said, holding his glass of tea in the air. He shot Heidi a knowing look before taking a sip.

"This is just..." Maxine started before Heidi interrupted her.

"Mom, could I actually talk to you for a second?" She tilted her head towards the kitchen, indicating she wanted to speak privately to her mom.

"Honey, we're all family now. What you say to me can be said to all of us."

Olivia and Arnald went stiff at her comment.

Heidi has expressed how often conversations between her, and her mom often turned into arguments. And while I've only experienced that once before, it didn't end well.

When Heidi didn't respond, Maxine asked, "What's wrong?"

"Nothing." Heidi shook her head. Her expression showed she was somewhere in her mind. She was silent for another beat before she looked at me, then at her sister, who I realized still had a hand on her shoulder. She then looked at my parents, almost apologetically. Her gaze narrowed and landed back on Maxine, "But I'd like to set some ground rules. I love you. And I know everything you do, and *say*, comes from a place of love. However, my relationship with Duncan is just that. Mine. It is not for you to tell me when or *if* we should or shouldn't get married. It's not for you to tell me how I should or shouldn't handle this relationship."

Maxine looked as if she was going to interject but Heidi didn't give her a chance.

"I promise, if I need advice, you will be the first person I come to. But you have to give me space to live my life the way I want to live it."

Heidi's posture remained tall, ready to defend her demand. Olivia and Arnold were still bracing for impact. My parents sat silently, waiting for the situation to unfold. They'd be ready to deescalate the situation if needed. They were good at that. Never judging. Just willing to help if needed.

Maxine was silent for longer than I anticipated. "You're absolutely right," she finally said. "I promise that I will try my hardest not to offer my unsolicited advice. I will work on giving you the space you need to build your life your way. I can't promise I'll be perfect, but I will try my best."

Arnold's gaze shifted to Olivia then bounced between Heidi and Maxine. Even I knew to hold my breath after that response. Maxine has feigned understanding before.

"Thank you…" Heidi's words sent a wave of relief through the room only for it to be snatched back. "Which leads me to my next topic."

*Oh shit.*

"– I took the job at the institute."

A range of emotions flashed across Maxine's face, and once again, Heidi made no show of backing down. I guess if she was removing the band aid, she might as well rip it all the way off.

"Oh. Th – that's great, honey. I will miss you."

"The good news is," Heidi assuaged. "I don't have to move. I will have to travel some, but I will continue to live here. But, it's a lot to explain right now and I really just want to get home and lay down."

"Okay, sweetheart," Arnald spoke, no doubt wanting to wrap up before things escalated. "Today has certainly been eventful." He stood, prompting Heidi to stand too. Arnald pulled her into a tight hug. "I'm happy for you. And I'm so very proud of you."

I couldn't see Heidi's face, but I could see her shoulders relax under her dad's words.

Maxine had made her way to Heidi next, also pulling her into a hug. "Yes, we're both very happy for you. I'll check in on you tomorrow, okay?" Heidi nodded in response.

We said our goodbyes to my parents next. My

mom had a permeant smile fixed to her face as she said, "Good for you, Honey."

"Thanks, Mom." She wrapped me in a hug, and it felt like weight had been lifted from both of our shoulders. She was genuinely happy for us.

I turned to my dad who had joined my mom as he said, "Watch out for each other." He looked between me and Heidi. "Not everyone is as lucky to have what the two of you have. You have to cherish it." It felt as if my dad's words carried a hidden meaning. Heidi and I both nodded, but Heidi had a look on her face that told me she knew what he meant.

"We will, Dad."

"I know you will. It's just my job to remind you." His hug was strong like his spirit, but fragile like his being.

This was part of the reason why I didn't want to keep my relationship with Heidi a secret anymore. My parents, although not my birth parents, had always been a source of comfort for me. They loved me when no one else did. They worked tirelessly to help me heal from my unknown past and they continued to place effort into ensuring I had a healthy and bright future. Coming clean to them, and everyone, about being with Heidi was my way of thanking them.

I know I wasn't perfect, and I still hadn't figured out the unknowns of my past, but it was time I moved forward with my life. My only hope was that whatever was hidden within the darkness of my memories, Heidi would still love me despite the truth.

I hoped that *I* would still love me.

# Chapter 6

## Duncan

Waking up the following morning, one of the weights I once carried in my chest had finally dissolved. I loved Heidi. I had always loved her. Now that our families knew we were together, I could wear that love freely in public.

Years back, we were the talk of the town when we went on a few dates. I had hoped to rekindle what we once had, but her apprehension was obvious. I couldn't blame her. I hadn't given her a reason to feel anything else towards me. Now that she had graciously given me another chance, I didn't want to screw it up.

But I need to be whole. A piece of me was still missing and the only way to find it was by confronting my past. I needed to remember what happened all those years ago before the Johnsons saved me from foster care. I didn't know it at the time, but I eventually learned that most children age out of foster care without ever finding a family to love them. I would forever be grateful for them taking me in, loving me like I was theirs, and bringing me to her.

I'll never forget my first day at school here in Mount Hopewell. Heidi's brunette hair was long and braided in pig tails. Her yellow dress drew my attention to her immediately. It was the same day I decided yellow would be my favorite color. And as far as I was concerned, it was the day I became real. The short years before her were a smear in my memory.

Any knowledge I did have before that time in my life came from my parents. For my fifteenth birthday they gave me a box filled with items from a childhood before them. The contents didn't mean anything to me then, and they hadn't meant anything to me since. Even so, I had never been able to discard the items. Naturally, I had questions about my birth parents, but the Johnsons didn't have any information about who they were. I never cared enough to look further for them since they didn't care enough to keep me to begin with.

I walked to my closet. From the top shelf, I pulled the dusty, shoe-box-sized box down and brought it with me to the living room. Unfolding the top flaps, I pulled out each item and placed them on the coffee table in front of me.

A small red toothbrush. A medium sized river rock. An unknown action figurine that I didn't recognize from any cartoon or comic. And a photo of a house that was cut from a newspaper. No caption to accompany the photo, but on the back was a portion of an article about a tornado destroying a neighborhood called the Medow Estates. I took my time looking over every object before closing my eyes, wishing a memory to come forward.

But nothing came.

Frustrated, I placed all the items back in their box and shoved it under the coffee table. I'd put it away later. For now, I needed to see my girl.

She didn't want me staying over with her last

night. She hadn't been feeling well and didn't want to share her germs with me. I tried to tell her that I wasn't worried about her germs, that I was tougher than they were. She let out a small laugh when she heard that one, and I thought she was about to give in but ultimately, she said she was worried more about my dad getting sick. She was worried if I were to get sick, I could somehow pass it off to him. It only made my heart stretch, becoming more filled with even more love for her.

Deciding that I wanted to bring her lunch while she was at work, I headed to the kitchen. I made two B.L.T.s, warmed up a bowl of chicken noodle soup, and grabbed a pack of saltines before packing the items away. I grabbed a couple of blankets from the linen closet and the lunch I packed before heading out the door.

"Heidi, you have a visitor!" Olivia hollered toward the back office as I entered the General Store.

I laughed at her teasing tone, "Hey, Olivia."

Heidi emerged from the back office hunched over slightly. A weak smile grew on her face when she saw me. "You might not want to get too close. I'm not feeling much better today than I was last night."

"Yeah. And she won't go home," Olivia chimed in.

"Well, it comes in waves, so at least it's not constant. I don't want to leave you here by yourself. Especially when I won't be here tomorrow."

"Heidi, the rush is over for the day. I can manage the rest of the day, and tomorrow, on my own. Please just take care of yourself and stop being so damn stubborn."

"Don't pay her any mind," Heidi said eyeing her sister before turning her attention back to me, smiling through her discomfort. She looked exhausted. "So, what brings you by?"

Before I could answer, Olivia interjected, "He's here to take you home. Aren't you, Duncan?" I looked back at her, her eyes serious, urging me to take Heidi home to rest. I turned back to Heidi, she stood, still hunched, waiting for me to confirm or deny her sister's claim.

"Yep. That's exactly it. That's why I'm here." Normally, I wouldn't insert myself between the two of them for any degree of disagreement, but Heidi didn't look well. Heidi started to roll her eyes, and I knew all too well she was ready to argue her stance. "And I'm not taking 'No' for an answer," I said firmly. It was my job to make sure she was taken care of, so she might as well get used to it now.

Heidi's hazel eyes flashed with emotion. I readied myself for her resistance, thinking she was going to object because she was worried about my dad, I also added, "And I will try my damnedest to avoid your germs."

Heidi was not the type of woman who liked to be told what to do. She stood there for a while, looking between me and her sister, likely contemplating her decision. "Okay," she finally gave in.

"Okay?" Olivia asked. Surprised – just as much as I was – that Heidi agreed.

Heidi's eyes never left mine as the corners of her mouth hinted at a smile, "Yeah. Take me home."

She trusted me. She trusted my word.

Heidi slowly turned towards the office. "Let me

just grab my stuff."

"No, I'll grab it." Still holding the large lunchbox packed with the food I made earlier, I passed her on my way to the office to gather her belongings. "Got your purse and jacket. Anything else?" Heidi shook her head. "Okay, let's get you home then." I tossed her jacket over my arm that was holding my lunchbox and now her purse and wrapped my free arm around her waist, guiding her to the door. "I'll come grab your car later," I said to her. She nodded softly and wrapped her arm around me, allowing me to support her as we walked.

"I hope you feel better. Call me if you need anything," Olivia said to Heidi before mouthing "Thank you" to me on our way out.

Back at Heidi's house, I set her up on the couch in the living room before bringing our lunch out. "Are you hungry? I made us some B.L.T.s and soup in case you might prefer something easy on your stomach."

"Yes, thank you," she said as I handed her a napkin and the plate with the B.L.T. I sat the bowl of soup and crackers on the table in front of her. "I take it this is why you really stopped by the store earlier?" she asked before taking a bite of her sandwich.

"Yeah, and I wanted to see how you were feeling."

Heidi's cheeks puffed out abruptly. Tossing the plate and throwing the banket off her, she covered her mouth and ran off down the hallway, disappearing into her room. I followed behind her and found her hunched over the toilet throwing up. I made myself busy dampening a washcloth with cold water. Pulling her hair back, holding it with one hand, I placed the cold rag on the back of her neck with the other.

Heidi spit into the toilet one last time before flushing and sitting back against the wall, bringing her knees in close to her chest, wrapping her arms around her knees and laying her head in her arms. I sat down beside her, hoping she wouldn't notice how close I was and lecture me about her germs. "I am so sorry you had to see that," she said with muffled words.

"Heidi, there's no need to apologize. Just let me help you." I rubbed the top of her back trying to comfort her. "What do you need right now?"

She sat quietly for a moment before tilting her head up slightly, peaking at me with one eye. "Some water?"

"Done." I quickly left for the kitchen, filled a glass with water and grabbed the saltines I packed earlier, and returned to the bathroom. Taking my seat back on the floor next to her, I handed her the glass of water and opened the saltines. "These will help calm your stomach."

Her eyes watered as she looked up to me, "Thank you."

I kissed her forehead, "Any time, baby." We sat there together as she nibbled on a few crackers and drank her water. "Feeling any better?"

"A little, but I'm going to lay down for a bit."

"Okay." I helped her up and put her into bed. I refilled her glass of water and sat it along with the crackers on her nightstand. "I'm going to get your car from the store, and I'll be back."

"You really don't have to do that, Duncan. I can get it later."

"I know you can, but I'm going to do it for you. All you need to do is rest." I kissed her forehead again, and she closed her eyes.

"Duncan," she pulled the covers in tighter to her chest, "I love you."

She didn't see the grin split my face when I replied, "And I love you."

*** 

Arriving at the store, I popped inside briefly to let Olivia know I was picking up Heidi's car. She asked for an update on how Heidi was feeling and looked concerned when I told her. "Will you be staying with her tonight?" Olivia asked.

"I will if she wants me to."

"I think it'll be good if you did. Will you ask her to call me when she wakes up please?"

"Sure thing."

When I arrived back at Heidi's house, I discovered she was fast asleep. I decided to head over to my house to pack a bag just in case she wanted me to stay over tonight. I left her a note telling her I'd be back and to call her sister if she woke up before I got back.

Back at my house, I spotted the box of forgotten things still under my coffee table. I decided to take the items out one more time, hoping a memory would become dislodged. This time, I focused on the newspaper clipping of the house. The black ink the image was printed in left most details indistinguishable. The only noteworthy thing about this house was its raised porch.

# Chapter 7

## Heidi

*I looked around the once cluttered apartment, no more beer bottles or cans were strewn across the floor.*

*Eirc was irritable when I Connected with him tonight but once I was able to help him calm down, he agreed to let me help him clean up. "What are you thinking about?" I had returned from the kitchen and saw him, sitting on the futon, staring blankly through the floor.*

*He was silent for a moment before answering. "I'm thinking about my daughter. I'm thinking about how weak I am. I'm thinking about..." His lips trembled, garbling his words as he attempted to speak through the emotion.*

*"Eric, I don't think you're weak." I moved from the doorway of the kitchen to the seat next to him. "I think you're incredibly strong, and brave, for being here. You sought treatment because you want to be better for your daughter. She's lucky to have a dad who is willing to do the hard work to become healthy."*

*"This is my fourth attempt at sobriety," he scoffed, shaking his head in disagreement. Tears spilled slowly from his lost blue eyes. "If I was so strong, it would have stuck by now."*

*"That may be true for some people, but everyone's journey to sobriety looks different. How*

*about we look at your previous attempts at sobriety as practice? I'm sure you learned healthy habits that you can use every day, right?" Eric nodded. "Good. So, now, we're going to add another skill to that practice. Graham mentioned that previously, you were able to remain sober as long as you avoided places or situations where alcohol was present. So instead of avoiding places and situations, we're going to avoid the alcohol specifically."*

*Eric sniffed through his tears, preventing them from falling faster as he shook his head.*

*"And in the end, you'll have an arsenal of healthy habits and practices to lean on daily," I reminded him quickly. His reason for sobriety was worthy and I'd be dammed if he failed. I sat quietly as Eric worked through the last of his tears and dried his face with the bottom of his tee shirt.*

*Eric exhaled raggedly, "Okay, I'm ready."*

***

Later that morning, I entered the lobby of the Keller Institute with an occupied mind. Last night's dream with Eric felt positive and productive. I was looking forward to discussing his progress with Graham. I was also going to complete my onboarding and become an official employee of the Keller Institute. What had me mostly distracted was the conversation I had with my sister on the drive over.

A smooth and familiar voice distracted my thoughts. Graham entered the lobby from the hallway that led to the offices on the main floor. "Good morning, Heidi." Seeing him in person was not the same as seeing him during a Connection. My stomach was doing flips with the way his bronzed skin contrasted beautifully with the white of his shirt, the way his smile and dark eyes warmed a room. I suddenly found it hard to swallow.

"Hi, Graham."

"How was your drive?"

"Good," was all I could manage to say. The nausea had returned.

"Good," he said with a charmed grin and a nod. "Please, follow me to my office."

We exited the lobby to the main hall. The office that once belonged to Dr. Keller had been cleared of all her belongings and the name tag on the door had been removed.

"We're looking to hire another doctor," Graham said as he opened the door to his office. "We've had some impressive candidates and we're hoping to make a final decision soon."

"We're?" I asked as I entered his office and took a seat.

"Me and the rest of the medical staff. It's important they have a say in who replaces my mother." He shut the door behind him and sat in the chair opposite mine.

Over the next two hours, I updated him on my interaction with Eric and we discussed my employment with the Keller Institute. We also discussed the training and certifications I would need to complete over the next couple of weeks. Thankfully, only one was in person and I would come back next week to complete it. My job would be to act as a recovery coach for patients who required additional support outside of traditional treatment.

My interaction with patients would mostly be through dreams. After any interaction with a patient, I was to update their patient portal – which was a secure site that housed patient details – with notes of our interaction. This would help Graham, or any other doctor the patient may be seeing, continue to foster a safe and conducive environment for healing from any addiction or anxiety.

I was beyond excited to be a part of this place. To be a part of something that helped people. To finally have a meaningful job was a literal dream come true. All that was left to do was to find a way to tell my parents about what my job actually entailed.

"Any other questions?" Graham asked.

"No. But I know how to get in touch if I do," I chortled.

A second of silence passed before my next words slipped past my lips. "Have you talked to her? Your mom." I clarified.

Graham nodded his head slightly. "Only once. I visited her after I buried my father." Graham cleared his throat and made a sweeping motion over his knee. "It was difficult to be in the same room as the woman, so I made sure our meeting was curt. She advised that her charges now included murder. The officer I spoke to said her attempted murder charge was amended and changed to murder because my father ultimately died as a result of what she did."

"I'm sorry," I said softly. "And I'm sorry that I didn't check in on you after that night. I know it wasn't easy saying goodbye to both your parents."

"I appreciate that. But the truth is, I lost them both

a long time ago."

My heart broke for Graham. My parents, mostly my mom, could be a bit of a nuisance, but I didn't know what I'd do without them. "Have you talked to Detective Reid since that night?"

"Yeah. He followed up with me the day after my mother's arrest but said he'd be in touch if he needed anything. You?"

"Not since he told me he'd likely have questions about this 'so-called ability' of mine." It was obvious Detective Reid was skeptical about how we knew all the details about her attempt to murder her husband. Thankfully she confessed but I had a feeling Detective Reid would not be easily appeased with just her confession.

Graham strummed his fingers on his knees. "So, you and Duncan…" His cocoa-colored eyes caressed my features, causing the memory of his touch to prick my senses.

My body shifted, trying to conceal the quiver that ran through me. "What about us?"

"Are you two together?'

"Yes. Why –"

"And you're happy?"

"Yes?" His candid questions caught me off guard.

"Mhm." He crossed his right rankle over his left knee. "I meant what I said. The apartment below mine is yours. If you want it."

"Graham, I…"

A knock sounded from the door before the brunette receptionist poked her head in. Annie, I think her name was? "Dr. Graham, your patient is here for intake evaluation. Do need me to reschedule?"

"No, that's alright. Please escort her to the Session Space and I will be in momentarily." The receptionist nodded and retreated down the hall towards the lobby. *Dr. Graham.* It never occurred to me that he was Dr. Keller too, technically. He must go by Dr. Graham so the patients could distinguish between which 'Dr. Keller' they would be meeting with.

"Thank you for your time today," I said, trying to regain some sort of balance from the last few minutes. "I will see my way out." I stood and began gathering my belongings.

Graham stood too. "Would you like to meet the patient? You could sit in on the evaluation, and I can introduce you."

Despite my wanting to put some space between Graham and I, I didn't want to pass up the opportunity, so I agreed. "Yeah. Okay, sure."

# Chapter 8

## Heidi

Graham gathered his pad and pen from his desk and motioned for me to follow him into the hallway. He gave me a brief update on the potential patient on our way.

"Good afternoon, Miss Fletcher," Graham said as we entered the Session Room. Extending his hand towards the blonde woman waiting on the couch, he introduced us. "I'm Dr. Graham and this is my colleague, Heidi Miller. She is our newest recovery coach and will be a beneficial resource in your recovery if you find yourself needing extra support."

"Hi Tawny. It's nice to meet you." I responded with a gentle handshake and smile.

"It's nice meet the two of you too," Tawny said almost shyly.

"Did you find your way okay?" Graham asked as we took our seats opposite the same indigo tufted couch I sat on just weeks ago.

"Yes. Thank you."

"Wonderful." Graham readied his pen. "Okay, Tawny. Want to tell us a little more about what brings you in today?"

"Yes." Tawny's gaze was fixed on her twiddling hands in her lap. She took a shaky breath and brought her gauze up. "It might sound a little juvenile, but I've been experiencing night terrors that someone is following me."

I felt the breath in my chest seize, hitched with worry.

"Have you experienced paralysis during any of these nightmares?" Graham asked, concern laced his question.

He must have wondered the same thing I did – *Could there be someone else out there capable of what Graham's dad was capable of?* Mr. Keller trapped Graham and I in a Connection for over three days.

Graham was already unconscious for a whole night by the time Dr. Keller begged for my help. She took me back to his apartment where nurses kept us under constant supervision while we were sleeping. When I Connected with Graham, he was locked in the gray room, the air slowly being stolen from our lungs. In that moment, with my last breath, I apologized. To him and to his dad for failing them both. And to Duncan, because I never gave us a second chance and we'd never know what our love would have looked like.

Thankfully, the sincerity in my voice cracked Mr. Keller's hardness and he lifted his walls, allowing light and air back into the gray room before completely pulling us into his consciousness. He had worried so much that his wife would try and conduct Connection experiments on him, that he held his conscious mind closed and locked up tight. Threatening to unknowingly suffocate and paralyze anyone who tried to Connect with him.

"No. I don't think so," Tawny replied.

I saw the subtle shift in Graham's posture as he relaxed. I did too. Being trapped in a paralyzing

Connection was an experience I never wanted to endure again.

Tawny went on to explain that these night terrors made dealing with her existing anxiety nearly impossible. "I know these are just dreams," she said embarrassed, "but every time I think about getting ready to leave the house, I start imagining the dream all over again. Some days it's so bad I can't even leave the house. I've missed several days of work this past month. I almost didn't make it to this appointment. But I'm exhausted from living this way." She pressed her fingertips to her temples and took a breath.

Graham flicked his eyes to his notes and scribbled something. "The events in your dreams, have they only happened in your dreams or have any scenarios been lived experiences?"

Tawny bit the inside of her lips. "They're lived experiences."

Again, Graham etched something in his notes. "Would you feel comfortable sharing more details on the incident?"

Tawny sat silent for a moment, still chewing on the inside of her bottom lip before slightly nodding.

"When I was eleven, walking home from school, a stranger attacked me from behind. He pushed me so hard that I fell and hit the broken sidewalk beneath me. I saw a large black boot plant itself beside me as hands wrapped around my neck and squeezed tightly. My vision had started to go dim when I heard a car horn honk frantically, pulling me back to consciousness. The man ran off. Unfortunately, he was never caught."

"How did you cope with what happened?"

"I was in therapy for many years afterwards. I learned to work through the anxiety and paranoia of an imminent attack." Tawny wiped her palms against her denim clad knees. "I was doing fine until the night terrors began." She bit the inside of her bottom lip and held it that way.

Graham must have sensed her hesitancy. He offered an encouraging nod. When she didn't respond, he asked, "Did anything unusual happen prior to when the terrors began?"

"A few weeks ago, as I was leaving work, I couldn't shake this eerie feeling that I wasn't alone. I had felt like that every day that week."

"How about in the last few days, when you do leave your home. Does it feel like someone is watching you then?"

Tawny shook her head.

Graham scribbled more notes. "Is there anything else you'd like to tell us about?"

Her hesitation returned and her eyes turned sad.

"This is a safe space. You are free to tell us anything that you're comfortable with sharing. You are also free to maintain your privacy if that's what you'd prefer. As long as you're honest about the information you do share, we can work through the rest."

Tawny nodded. "Okay." She resumed chewing on the inside of her lips, her breathing fell with an equal rhythm. Almost as if each inhale and each exhale lasted the same amount of time. "I don't have anything else to share. I just need help handling my anxiety. I don't want to be held prisoner to it or these nightmares anymore."

Graham made a quick note on his pad before discussing her options for treatment and explained how dream therapy could be beneficial for her.

The Institute had five rooms for patients who opted for or required in-patient treatments. For patients who didn't need to stay overnight, they would come in for weekly or even daily sessions.

At the end of the session, Graham escorted her back to the lobby to schedule further treatment and for her to complete additional intake forms.

Upon Graham's return from the lobby, he explained that Annie would schedule Tawny's appointments for treatment. If during her treatment, it was determined that she needed additional support from me, Graham would update me on her progress and how to help her further. "At this time, Eric is our only patient who requires your help."

I nodded my head, relieved his professionalism remained. "Would I need to sit in on all patient evaluations?"

"It's not necessary. I will provide you with any and all relevant details required to make your assistance effective."

"Understood." I stood and pulled my purse strap over my shoulder. "Is there anything else I could help with before I go?"

Something wicked flashed behind his soulful brown eyes, sending a warm flutter down my spine. "No. We've covered everything we needed to today. I will update Eric's chart with steps for you to focus on next."

"Okay," I wasn't sure if I should leave with a hug

or a handshake. I opted for an awkward wave instead. "I'll check in later tonight." I tucked my hair behind my ear and headed for the door where he still stood. Graham offered just enough space for me to slip between him and the doorframe without touching, but close enough to feel the heat of his sculpted body.

I didn't turn to look back as I willed my feet to carry me to the lobby, but I felt his eyes lingering on me, watching me until I exited the hallway.

The fresh air enveloped me in its cleansing embrace as I exited the Keller Institute. My thoughts swirled with furry as I started my car. "One thing at a time," I said to myself. "I had other matters to attend to."

# Chapter 9

## Duncan

The day dragged slowly, as if the hands of time slugged through molasses. After spending most of my day helping the guys haul materials into the various storage buildings on the lot, I decided to finalize our delivery schedule. With our recent acquisition of our latest contract, the schedule had been fairly easy to establish. I also arranged a partnership with the only other lumber yard in the state to provide any additional materials we may require for any given delivery. Now that Ronny's deliveries would be local, they would also be more frequent.

The property developer we were now contracted with had several projects throughout several cities in the state. Their main office was located in Easton City, and I would travel there for any meetings or contact amendments and extensions that may be needed.

Too bad I didn't need to be in Easton City today. Heidi was there completing her onboarding requirements for the Keller Institute. I was happy for her, truly, but there was something untrustworthy about that Graham guy that had me on high alert. I didn't want to call it jealousy just yet, but whatever it was, it was a feeling I wasn't familiar with.

I sat, allowing myself to tune into the distant chatter from the crew, only being interrupted by the rev and whine of chainsaws as the metal teeth bit the wood. I could picture the size and cut of the wood just from the clattering that echoed when it was being loaded. For some people, this would be considered as a nuisance, or racket, but for me, this was the sound of home. The sound of pride. The sound of hard work, dedication, and family. It was often a solace that allowed me to get my thoughts in order.

Lately, and understandably, my thoughts were consumed with Heidi. Her love made me feel both brave and afraid. Brave enough to confront the past that remained hidden, but scared that once I remembered it, I wouldn't be able to keep her.

How's the saying go, it's better to have loved and lost, than to never have loved at all? Well, I call bullshit. Anyone who's ever been in love knows you'd be better off ignorant to its existence. Because once love has bitten you, spreading its infection through every vein in your body, you become incurable.

I'll forever regret breaking her heart. Never forgetting the betrayal in her eyes when I was too much of a coward to be honest with her back then.

When I first started school here in Mount Hopewell, I made friends easily, everyone was eager to accept the new kid. And even though this was a small town, no one treated me unfairly because I wasn't a true local. Or because I was the boy who forgot how to speak. No, this town spread gossip quicker than a wildfire, but when it came to me, I never heard an unkind word.

Most of my time was spent roughing it up with the other boys my age. But every now and then, Heidi would let me join her on her walks. Behind the school, there were several trials that students were allowed to walk. Whether it'd be for an outdoor assignment or for enjoyment, students were allowed to walk them whenever we wanted as long as it was before dusk. That's where Heidi spent most of her time.

She always talked about the adventures she'd go on once she grew up. She'd get far away from this tiny town and only miss it on Sundays. Except, back then, I didn't know about her dreams and how they dictated her thoughts. I only thought she had an overactive imagination.

Our weekly hikes together eventually turned into daily hikes and something special bloomed in the woods all those years ago. There on those trails, my feelings for her grew. My crush had gone from innocent daydreaming during class to borderline obsession. Anytime she was near me, my heart raced. My palms grew sweaty. If I had that kind of effect on her, she didn't let it show.

By the time we were fifteen, we would sneak off, away from the trails to our secret spot and make out. By the time we were seventeen, our kisses and heavy petting evolved into the first adult decision we made. That warm July evening was the best and worst day of my life.

Her eyes winced suddenly before relaxing her expression, granting me permission. "Are you sure?" I asked her after my first careful thrust.

All signs of pain from her eyes melted away and her lips curved softly. "More than okay." Her hands found their way to my unkept curly hair and pulled me down for a kiss.

I continued my gentle strokes, in and out of her, coaxing her body to relax. Her eyes never left mine, pulling me deeper into her gaze. She bent her legs and spread them wider apart, allowing me to reach deeper into her core. Her back arched as her hips angled down, holding me completely captive by the raw beauty I had the privilege of witnessing. Watching Heidi Miller come around my dick for the first time was euphoric.

*My* first time was euphoric. When my eyes landed back on hers, I felt like I had purpose. To love her. To protect her. To make her smile every single day because when she did, I felt whole. Except, I wasn't whole. Something hideous, refusing to be discovered, lurked in the gaps of my mind.

"I love you, Duncan." Her voice rang in my mind, causing the memory to slice sharply though my heart. Her hazel eyes were round and doe like, peering up at me like I hung the stars and the moon. And that's when it hit me, a reminder, like a sudden sickness that dwelled deep in my mind and heart.

I was not worthy of love.

# Chapter 10

## Heidi

"I can't believe you're making me do this before everyone gets here."

"Because I know you. You'll be out there, your thoughts all scrambled up in your brain…" Olivia made claws with her hands and swirled them around in front of her, like she was washing an invisible head.

"My thoughts are already all scrambled up." I interrupted and mimicked her gesture. "I should've just rescheduled. Maybe it's not too late to call them."

Olivia's hands held my shoulders and stilled me. "Heidi, get. A. Grip." She put on her big sister voice. Which meant she was about to tell me something I probably wasn't going to like. "If I'm right, you're going to have to learn to be a lot less indecisive. You won't have the luxury of letting your thoughts get the best of you."

She was right. I didn't like it, but she was right. My thoughts could no longer just be about me. If two little pink lines showed up on this stick, they'd be about my baby.

I replaced the cap on the end of the pee stick and sat it on the back of my toilet. "How long do we have to wait again?" Nerves had already taken hold of me shaking my insides, making me feel queasy. How could I have missed the signs? Weren't women supposed to have some sort of sixth sense about this kind of thing?

"Three minutes."

"Ugh. That's so long!" I left the bathroom to take a seat at the foot of my bed. Just as my butt hit the mattress, I heard a knock at the door. I jumped up, panicked and flicked my eyes from the pregnancy test to Olivia.

"Go!" she yelled quietly, shooing me away.

I hurried my way to the front door, trying to calm the marathon rate of which my heart was beating. Taking a quick steadying breath, and cursing Olivia with it, I opened the door to greet my parents.

"Hello, sweat heart," my dad said with a hug.

"Hey, Dad."

"Hi, honey." Mom placed the palm of her hand on my cheek and looked affectionately at me before wrapping me in her embrace.

I hitched my eyebrow towards my hairline and looked at the side of her head, wondering where my mom had gone. "Hi, Mom?"

She didn't notice and happily made her way inside toward the kitchen as I closed the door behind her. "It smells good in here, Heidi," my mom complemented.

*Seriously, who is this woman?* "Thanks, Mom."

Dad wasted no time before finding him a spot on the couch and turning on the tv. I noticed Olivia wasn't anywhere in sight yet. Another knock at the door caused me to turn quick on my heel to answer it.

"Duncan…. Hi!" *Oh shit. Duncan.* My mind raced back to the pregnancy test in my bathroom. *Shiiiiiit.* Again, I cursed Olivia inwardly.

"Oh, Honey, there you are." I heard my mom say

from somewhere behind me. Tossing a glance over my shoulder, I saw that Olivia had enter the kitchen with Mom.

"Evening, Heidi," Duncan leaned down and planted a swift kiss on my cheek before coming in and greeting my dad. "Good evening, Arnold."

Shutting the door behind Duncan, I searched for my sister, finding her just inside the kitchen still. I widened my eyes at her, trying to communicate the question burning my mind. Her eyes flashed wide then looked left, indicating Mom was in earshot.

My shoulders slumped, weighed down with wondering. I'd just have to wait to go see for myself. Hearing my dad ask me a question snapped my posture back up right. "I'm sorry, what was that, Dad?"

"How was your trip to the city today? Was there a lot of traffic on the road?"

"Oh. Uh, no. Not too much."

"That's good. And everything went okay at the institute?"

I thought back to my interaction with Graham. I wasn't sure how he was able to switch between being a total flirt to being completely professional. My heart would never betray me the way my body tried to today. *Heidi, get. A. Grip.* Olivia's voice echoed from the corner of my mind. "It was good. And that's actually why I invited you and Mom tonight. I wanted to…to tell you about my job there."

The kitchen timer set off a shrill beep, "Supper's ready!" Olivia and I both called, trying to conceal our nervousness. I had hopped my awkward, apologetic, half grin would help me appear casual as I excused myself from the living room. The downward twitch of Duncan's eyebrows said it didn't.

Olivia and I both worked in the kitchen to get supper pulled together when another knock alerted us that Ronny had finally arrived. "I'll get it," Duncan hollered from the living room.

"Is there anything I can help either of you with?" Mom asked.

"Nope."

"Yeah, no. We're good, Mom."

Meatloaf, mashed potatoes, roasted broccoli, and dinner rolls lined the counter. Since my table was small and only sat four people, we decided the women would sit in the kitchen and the men could sit in the living room, in front of whatever sports station they were streaming.

Conversation over supper did little to ease the scrambling of my thoughts. I still hadn't had the chance to steal away to the bathroom to see if one line or two appeared. Olivia hadn't offered a hint or any indication of the results either.

All three men entered the kitchen with empty plates and placed them in the sink. Mom, Olivia, and I had only just finished our first serving a few minutes ago. My dad and the guys had already finished with seconds. I cleared the plates from the table and asked if everyone would join me in the living room.

I chose to tell everyone today because I had finally felt a little better than I had been the last two days. But that sick feeling had retuned.

Everyone found a seat in the living room, and I took a seat on the coffee table in front of the couch where my parents and Olivia sat. Olivia sat there for support, to remind me that I wasn't alone. She gave me a reassuring nod, and it was like she loaned me some of her confidence.

"First, I wanted to say thank you for everyone joining me this evening. As you all know, I recently accepted a job at the Keller Institute. What most of you don't know is what my job is." I sat, facing my parents, giving myself a quick internal pep talk before I let the truth spill out. "I am the Keller Institute's newest recovery coach. What that means is that I will act as support for any of our patients who need it." My words and their meaning went right over my parents' heads. They were nodding along, wanting to follow, but their eyes were devoid of comprehension.

"And you can do that from here?" Mom asked tentatively.

"Yes." On my way home from the city today, I rehearsed what I had planned to say to them a hundred times, but now, I was at a loss for words. How did I explain that their daughter had a unique ability? That involves my dreams, no less. To say my dreams had been a touchy subject my whole life was an understatement.

*Get. A. Grip.* Olivia's words whispered in the back of my mind once more. I felt both Olivia's and Duncan's gaze fall on me, urging me, supporting me. "Yes. I am able to do all of that from here because I do it all from my dreams."

My mom's expression turned to stone. Her lips pressed firmly in a line. I needed to convince her, and fast.

"Do you remember the winter I learned to ski? How the whole day before, no matter what I did, I couldn't seem to stay of my feet. But the next day, you took me back to the slopes and I didn't fall a single time." Recognition flashed behind my parents' eyes. Frustration accompanied my mom's expression. "And Michael. That's how I found him." I gathered my long hair and twisted it together before pulling it over my shoulder. My neck was getting hot under their pensive stares. "It wasn't just a hunch, Dad. I saw him. I – I found him in my dream. He told me his name and what happened. He told me he caught himself on the roots that protruded from the riverbank. That's how I knew where to look."

My dad's confusion turned to awe but I had yet to placate my mom. I turned to look over my shoulder and Ronny and Duncan, "That's how I knew about your dad and his diagnosis. He's the one who sent me to check on you," I said to Duncan. "Ronny did too, but your dad told me first." I turned back to face my mom, "And that's how my *silly* dream about witnessing a murder helped me put a very dangerous woman behind bars."

My mom gave me a lot of shit for looking into Whyatt's murder. In her defence, I didn't have proof that someone had died, and I didn't yet know his name. But she accused me of making up dreams just to feel important. And I needed her to know, that maybe I wasn't important, but my ability was. I would be able to help people because of it.

Silence filled the spaces between us. This information was not new to Duncan or Olivia. But I could feel the shock and bewilderment radiate off my parents and Ronny.

"So, are you a psychic?" Ronny asked, breaking

the silence with a little bit of humour in his tone.

I shook my head. "There's not a name for what I am perse, but there is for the ability. It's called Connecting. And all that means is that I can connect to other unconscious energies. Usually someone else who is also dreaming."

"So, you offer dream assistance?" Ronny asked, trying to grasp my explanation. I didn't blame him, I felt similarly when Dr. Keller tried to explain it to me.

I laughed and nodded because that's exactly what my job was. "I'm still learning to navigate them all, but each time, it's a little easier." I decided not to go too deep into all the details of Connecting with Mr. Keller. I explained to everyone, but mostly my parents, that I was able to Connect with him and that's how we go the truth about Dr. Keller. I also let my parents know that they may see a detective here if he decided to question Graham and I further about the night in question.

It didn't take long for my dad to come around, but my mom appeared to still have her reservations about it all. I was impressed, and thankful, that she held true to her word this time. Not offering her unwanted opinion on my life.

I had asked everyone to keep this between themselves, I didn't want to be the talk of the town, spending my time dodging questions from our nosey neighbors.

Mom managed to say a few, neutral words before she and Dad left for the evening. The night had gone better than I expected.

There was still one more matter I needed to attend to. I snuck away from the living room, leaving

Ronny, Duncan, and Olivia on the couch in front of the tv.

Nerves returned to my fingertips as I approached the pregnancy test that remained on the back of the toilet. I held it gingerly between my thumb and pointer finger and closed my eyes as I lifted it up, not yet ready to see.

"Congratulations," my sister whispered behind me.

My eyes flew opened at the declaration only to be met with twin pink lines.

# Chapter 11

## Duncan

Helping Heidi clean up the kitchen after supper, she was adamant that we stay the night at my house instead of hers. I didn't understand the urgency but as long as I was with her, I was sated. I didn't care who's house we stayed at. And although I had plans to take her straight to the bedroom once we arrived, I could tell her mind was already occupied.

Heidi always wore her thoughts in her expression. Not in a way that you could tell what she was thinking, just that her mind was hard at work, sorting and prioritizing what earned her attention, and what would have to wait. I tried to never push her to share when she got like that, but I was curious of all the thoughts occupying her mind. I wondered which ones owned her attention and which ones she cast aside.

We spent the rest of our evening laid up on the couch in front of the tv, watching one of the various streaming services I paid for. I was unable to focus on whatever it was she finally decided on, I was busy trying to tame my cock from growing. Her round ass was pressed to my front, causing my girth to thicken from the contact.

I wondered if she noticed when I flipped my length into my waistband and dug my hips into the back of the couch, trying to put any amount of distance between me and that perfect ass of hers. But the void had only existed for a moment before she backed further into me, rolling her hips slightly to push herself up towards me to position her head comfortably in the crook of my arm. Blood rushed to the head of my cock as it throbbed, beckoning for the warmth between her thighs.

Fortunately, and unfortunately, we both were wearing sweatpants to combat the chill that settled with the moon, but I couldn't help imagining how it'd feel to be naked, pressed flushed against her like this. The way I'd be able to wrap my arm around her, cupping her breast, holding her in place against my body. I'd tease a rosy peak with my eager thumb as it gently stroked the tender flesh. Her head would lean back onto me, allowing me to nip at the flesh between her neck and shoulder...

Her body rolled, turning her back to the tv she now faced me, interrupting the ardent scene unfolding in my mind. She looked at me with glossy hazel eyes, golds and greens becoming hidden beneath heavy eyelids. "You ready to go to bed? I don't think I'm going to be able to finish this," she said, slightly flicking her head back to gesture towards the movie.

"I'm ready if you are." I dipped my chin to kiss her forehead. She smiled.

Her arms reached up past her head, and her legs shot down and back. Slightly arching her back as her hips pushed towards me, towards the throbbing that hid beneath my waist band, as she stretched. The hem of her tee shirt rose just a little, exposing the bare skin of her waist and stomach. I swallowed hard, pushing down the desire to tease the exposed skin with my lips and tongue. She brought her arms and legs back in towards her body and she curled against me. She buried her face in my chest and took a deep breath in. I stroked her hair against her back as she stayed curled next to me, breathing deeply. She turned her head and looked up at me. Her eyes searched my face, but for what I wasn't sure.

"Are you okay?"

Heidi's expression morphed before I could decipher it. "Yeah. Just a lot on my mind."

I nodded and continued to stroke my hand down her back. I figured as much. Especially after having to explain to her parents about her job at the institute. I was honestly surprised Maxine remained calm but was grateful she did for Heidi's sake.

Once we made our way to the bed, she climbed in and crawled over to the side farthest from the door. Her head hit the pillow and her eyelids slammed shut. I climbed in and scooted closer to her, laying face to face. I threw my arm across her legs that were balled up close to her chest. Immediately she rolled away from me and pulled my arm over her stomach to hug her as she backed into me once again. I extended my arm for her to lay her head on, our bodies flush against each other, I fought the images from earlier.

"I love you," she said softly.

I smiled and gently squeezed her closer to me, "I love you, too."

***

*Heavy footfalls vibrated the featureless walls, like lightning striking too close. Grunts and snarls reverberated thought the infinite stretch of the dim hall. The sliding and shattering of glass in the*

*distance caused my head to swivel, searching*
*frantically for the direction it came from. I heard the*
*sharp crack of skin-to-skin contact. Another grunt. A*
*whimper. A thwack.*

*Sick forced its way up my throat. Sweat pricked*
*my forehead. My vision went hazy.*

*Thwack.*
*Thwack.*
*Thud.*
*Silence.*

I sprang upright, almost like my heart had
pounded too hard against the mattress beneath me,
causing my chest to catapult forward. My head
continued its swivel before realizing the only sounds I
heard now came from Heidi breathing softly beside
me.

My eyes travelled down the curve of her body, her
back still towards me. I took note of how peacefully
she slept. Her breaths were a steady lull, easing my
heartrate back to normal. I dragged my hands through
my hair, searching my mind for an explanation of
what the fuck that dream was about.

Something familiar in the corner of my mind
echoed, but it was too far away to be intelligible.
With an uneasy feeling seated in my gut, I carefully
got out of bed and started to make my way towards
the hallway. I felt compelled to take a look around the
house, ensuring everything was as it should be. The
windows in every room were locked, as were both
doors.

I was in the minority, likely the only resident here
who locked up each night. Most people felt it wasn't
necessary, with the exceptions of those who owned

businesses. Even though our town saw tourists year-round, the residents never felt threatened enough to lock their houses at night. By all accounts, this was likely the safest town in the country. Still, the notion had never settled with me, and I ensured my doors and windows were locked every night.

I took a quick peek out of the living room window that offered the best view of the driveway. The moonlight illuminated the view well enough for me to discern any shadows that may have been lurking. Only my truck and Heidi's car sat in my driveway.

Finally returning to my bedroom, satisfied that the house was secure, Heidi was still in the same position I left her in. I was grateful my startle hadn't disturbed her. Bad dreams hadn't been an issue for me since I was a child, and this one rattled me. I hoped this was nothing more than a random disruption to my otherwise solid sleeping habits.

Otherwise, I'd need to make sure I figured it out without alarming Heidi. If my dream had anything to do with my past, I didn't want her anywhere near it until I understood what I was dealing with.

# Chapter 12

## Heidi

"How long are you going to keep it from him?" Olivia's expression harboured concern and criticism but her tone made no effort to conceal it.

"Shhh! What if someone walked in hearing you talk like that," I hissed. Normally, working in such a small space with my sister wasn't an issue. However, today I would love to have had a little distance from her.

"When I said you didn't have to rush into any decision, I didn't mean to take a week. I meant take a day or two to figure out how you're going to tell him." Olivia paced the short distance between the counter and office, irritated, her hand on her forehead. "Your appointment is tomorrow. Did you plan to go without him? Don't you think he'd like to be there to hear the heartbeat for the first time?"

My eyes like daggers pierced her, killing the line of questioning. So much had happened in this last week that I wasn't sure how or if I should tell Duncan about this baby. Well, not *if*, but when and how to tell him.

His childhood was a touchy subject. He didn't talk about it. Ever. But his dreams lately have alluded to something tragic that I couldn't help but to worry and wonder if the two were related. I'm not certain that they're tied to his past but whatever they're about, they have him shaken. Not that he showed any trepidation during our day to day, but I knew too well that our dreams held the truth we didn't always see while conscious.

I stayed true to my promise and made Eric my priority when Connecting. He had made steady progress with this past week and his attitude had changed drastically. Positivity and perseverance looked good on him, and Graham agreed.

My heart was full. I was helping someone make a difference in their life.

However, whenever our Connections ended, I would notice a lingering green haze. Each time they had led me to Duncan. I was with him in an obscure hallway, panic visibly displayed across his face. Any recognition of me being with him was lost in the chaos he was focused on.

The night I found out I was pregnant was the same night I first Connected with him during that dream. I waited for him to mention it to me the morning after, but he never did. At first, I thought maybe he didn't recall the dream, but he's had the same dream every night since, and he still hadn't said anything to me. I ultimately concluded that he either hadn't noticed me and didn't want to tell me about them, or he in fact didn't recall it after he woke up. Either way, it felt intrusive to ask him about it.

I wanted to help, but I didn't want to rush him or intervene with what he was dealing with internally. But I didn't like watching him deal with his demons alone. I was able to lean on him when I needed him. I wanted to provide him the same love and support.

"Olivia, there's just a lot going on right now."

"Like what, Heidi?" Olivia crossed her arms

across her chest, "Has Detective Reid reached out, asking for more details about the investigation?" I shook my head. "Are your responsibilities at the institute overwhelming you?" I shook my head again. I watched her eyes narrow with intensity, "Then what the hell could be preventing you from keeping the truth from him?"

I stared at her from my seat behind the counter. She would only think the truth was an excuse.

"Answer me, Heidi! Even you have to know this is wrong to keep from him. Not to mention the rest of his family, and ours, who would undoubtedly be elated when the find out."

"I'm scared." My voice was barely a whisper. Before I could finish, I saw Olivia frown with disbelief.

"Scared of what? Heidi, what aren't you telling me?"

I never told her, or anyone, about Duncan and me. About how we lost our virginities to each other at seventeen. Or how I told him that I loved him, and he completely walled himself off afterwards.

I had scared him away. With just my words. What if this would push him away for ever? What if this time he'd wall himself off so tight that he'd disappear from not just my life, this baby's life too? I don't know how I'd recover from that. It had taken him nearly ten years to come around to the idea of loving me. I wouldn't have ten more years for him to get comfortable with becoming a father.

That and the fact these disturbing dreams he'd been having lately made me feel unsteady. If he remembered them, I was sure he'd be trying to unravel them in his mind. I worried that, coupled with the news of an unexpected pregnancy, would push him away from me completely.

"What if he decides he doesn't want to be a father?" I finally acknowledged out loud. "The last time I dropped a bomb on him, he got distant, turning his back on the relationship I thought we had.

"What do you mean?" Some of Olivia's frustrations had dissipated, but she remained standing with her hand on her hip.

I signed and swivelled to face her directly. "Okay but promise you won't get mad." Her eyebrow arched, ready to protest. "Olivia, promise me you won't get mad." She never reacted well when I withheld information from her, especially secrets like this.

She rolled her eyes, "I'll try."

Good enough. "Duncan was my first."

"Your first what…" Her eyes widened with the realization.

"And I was his."

She had to sit down for that revelation.

"We were seventeen. It wasn't a rushed or rash decision. It's what we both wanted. Or I thought we both wanted it." My heart broke for seventeen-year-old me, how hopeful I felt in the moment before telling him that I loved him. Then how quickly hope turned to embarrassment and confusion. "I told him that I loved him for the first time too." I looked away from Olivia's emotional expression. "We were never the same after that."

"And you're worried he'll react the same way once you tell him you're pregnant." Olivia sat in silence for a moment before allowing the corner of her mouth to curve upward. "You know, Duncan is crazy about you. Even back then it was obvious. And I say this, not to dismiss how he handled the situation, but I'm sure he had his reasons."

Dumbfounded, I slapped the side of my thigh in exacerbation, "Olivia, how could you defend him?" Her comment, sounding much like something our mom would say, surprised me. I couldn't keep the hurt from my voice.

"I'm not saying you deserved it. And how he handled the situation was complete shit, but think about it. Duncan was never the type of kid to make irresponsible, cruel, or intentionally immature decisions. He had always been more thoughtful than most boys his age."

Was Olivia right? I thought back to our childhood. When all the other boys our age were busy throwing frogs at each other and laughing whenever one smashed against someone, Duncan had tried to stop them. During our teenage years, whenever we'd sneak out to a bon fire, nearly everyone drank themselves to the brink of a blackout. But not Duncan. He had one, maybe two beers tops. For the few kids who had cars, he'd been sure to collect their keys from them and would return them the following day. And during his eighteenth birthday, when Sarah McRay made a spectacle of herself by trying to flirt with him, he had led her to the side of his parents' house, away from mostly everyone's view and politely told her "No thanks". I knew because I couldn't pull my eyes away from the commotion and I followed them when he led her away from the party.

I remember how my heart raced, sinking to my belly as I anticipated their next move. Instead, I witness the very popular, and by far the prettiest girl in our grade get rejected and storm off in a fit. Sarah wasn't accustomed to being told 'no'.

"Okay, so maybe you're on to something. But intentional or not, I still don't know why he ended things between us."

"It sounds like teenage Heidi needs some closure."

I smirked and rolled my eyes. "And how do I do that?"

"You're just going to have to ask him for it."

# Chapter 13

## Heidi

Repeatedly, I tried to play out the situation in my head, of how tonight was going to go. But no amount of prepping could sway the nerves that vibrated through my gut. Not only was I going to tell Duncan I was pregnant, but, like Olivia said, I needed closure.

Duncan's house had become familiar since I had been here for a week straight. I worried he'd find the pregnancy test in the trash at my house the night I found out, so I suggested we stay here instead, and I had been here ever since. Considering the state of his dreams lately, I wanted to be close in case he needed me.

I heard the water running from Duncan's bathroom as I made my way down the hallway. The clean earthy aroma of sandalwood filled my nostrils as I entered the bathroom's steamy embrace. Listening to the water rush down, spilling over his broad shoulders, down his firm chest and back, and eventually down to the appendage that was responsible for most, if not all, of my complete undoings.

I heard the squeak of the faucet knob as it rotated, turning off the water and pulling my attention back to the matter at hand. Duncan slid the shower curtain back, his tall, hard body glistened from the water that clung to his skin. Hell, I didn't blame it.

If my presence startled him, he didn't show it. Or maybe I didn't notice it. My eyes were somewhere south of his waist. Without haste, he stepped over the white acrylic wall of the tub before reaching for his towel and wrapping it around his waist. My frown was quickly erased with his lips as he closed the gap between us and pressed hungrily into me, pinning me between his erection and the wall. Just as I began to melt at his feet, he pulled away, looking almost apologetic when his green eyes fell to my lips. His thumb slid across my swollen bottom lip before creating a little space between us, regaining his composure. His smile and voice steady, trying to conceal the lust still present in his tone. "What's on your mind, babe?"

*How I should rip that towel off of you and drop to my knees.* I snapped my eyes up to his, trying to remember why I needed to talk to him. Oh, right! *I'm carrying your child.*

Nerves in my gut roared to life again, making the nausea return. I wasn't sure if it was because of the situation or the baby. Either way, I wouldn't be able to focus until he was better concealed. "Maybe put some pants on first." My eyes flicked from his face to the bulge threatening to undo the towel that hung sinfully low on his hips. A wicked grin formed on his lips before he winked and walked past me, exiting to his bedroom.

The lamp on his bedside table cast a soft ember glow between the four walls. I found my way to the king-sized bed that occupied the middle wall of his bedroom. His charcoal gray sheets had been pulled up and made before we left for work this morning. Each of the four pillows were returned to their respective places at the head of the bed near the shiny black pleather headboard.

He never had dirty clothes on the floor, and his black pressed wood dresser was never in disarray. In fact, all of his spaces were tidy and neat. Something I hadn't noticed before with the exception of his truck. Anytime I had been in it, it was always clean. Despite working around sawdust all day long, his truck never had any in it.

*Duncan took care of his things.*

He slid into a pair of sweatpants, sans his boxers, and took a seat next to me on the mattress.

I crossed my legs, fully facing him, doing my best not to reach out and drag my hand through his tuft of chest hair. I squared my shoulders and pulled myself together. "I need to know what happened between us. Before."

His eyes searched mine, looking for a clue to what I was referring to.

"That day in the woods. Our first time." Clarity and regret stretched across his handsome face. "Why did you leave me?"

Duncan stood, dragging his hand down his beard, contemplating my question. He looked as if his thoughts warred inside as he traveled the length of the bed.

"Duncan," I said softly. "I have to know. I have to know that this time won't be like that time."

Guilt shaped his face, and he returned back to his seat in front of me. "This time won't be like last time."

"How do I know that? How do I know that one

day you're not going to wake up and decide I'm not at all what you want?"

"Because Heidi, only a fool makes the same mistake twice."

"Duncan," my voice low, reminders of the hurt I felt back then came flooding to the forefront of my mind. I thought he loved me then, and he said he loved me now, but I couldn't take the chance of him changing his mind once he knew about this baby. I wouldn't put our child through that heartbreak. "I need you to let your walls down."

The moments of silence between us felt like it lasted for hours before Duncan finally spoke. "Can't you trust me on this, Heidi. Trust that I love you and I'm here to stay. I was a dumb ass kid before, not knowing what I had when I had it." He extended his legs in a V and pulled me closer, unfolding my legs and pulling me on top of him. Instinctively, I wrapped my arms around his neck, and his arm found their natural place around my hips. His erection was growing thick again, and my core responded stubbornly with a hungry ache.

"Duncan," I grew lightheaded as desire rushed through my veins. Fighting the urge to grind against him, I let the words slip harshly between my lips. "Does it have anything to do with the dreams you've been having?"

A wave of emotions rolled through Duncan's green eyes, his breath stilling in his chest. "Heidi, how do you know about my dreams?" His question was asking for an explanation, not the literal workings of how a Connection worked. Which meant he hadn't seen me any of the times I was there with him.

Which meant he purposefully kept them from me.

In those dreams, I could see the fear and terror etched across his face as he listened to the slaps, stomps, and thuds that played in a loop. All the while, perfectly concealing that fear while in my conscious presence. If he could keep a calm mask in place after all that, who's to say he's not doing it now?

Everything in my heart screamed that I was overreacting and that I should trust Duncan. Olivia was right, it was not in his nature to do things without careful intention. But Duncan was also right – only fools make the same mistake twice. And I didn't want to make the same mistake again.

I climbed off his lap, fury and anguish making my legs wobbly. My chest tightened as I tried to fill my lungs with a deep cleansing breath. My feet finally rooted securely on the floor. "How could you not see me? I was standing right there with you, each time. Why won't you let me help you? Why can't you let your walls down and let me *in*?"

Duncan stood too, his eyes looking at me and through me simultaneously. His gauze sent a blaze of heat up my neck which was quickly extinguished by the chills that followed immediately after. Seeing Duncan's raw emotions like this was a first for me. I didn't quite know what to expect from him, but I wasn't scared. I was sad. "Because this doesn't involve you. You need to stay far away from this."

Something terrible was locked deep inside and he was being foolish trying to handle it alone.

"If it involves you, it involves me. What if I told you to stay behind when we went to confront Dr.

Keller? What if I told you it was none of your business, that it didn't concern you?" I crossed my arms, arched my eyebrow, and cocked my head. "Would you have listened?"

I thought I saw concede in his eyes. If I did, it was only there until he blinked it away. He growled, keeping his words to himself, grabbed his keys from his nightstand and left the room. I followed quickly behind him, just to catch him at the front door, sliding his hoodie on.

"Where are you going?" I didn't close the gap between us like I wanted to. I was frozen, watching the man I loved, get ready to walk out on me again.

"I need to clear my head."

The door didn't slam but the sound of it was loud enough to shake my hollowing heart. I waited as I heard his truck crank and back out of the driveway. Tears from anger, sadness, and concern streamed down my face.

I showered and did my best to wash the emotion away. Once I crawled into bed, I tried to wait up for him, but my eyelids grew heavy. Sleep claimed me before Duncan returned home.

# Chapter 14

## Duncan

So many emotions rushed through me as I barreled towards my truck. Worry and embarrassment taking center stage. I started up my truck and peeled out of the gravel driveway. Hauling ass around the turns of the empty roads until I reached route 125.

I fought like hell not to retreat into the silenced darkness of my mind. The same silence that consumed me as a child, then again after learning of my dad's cancer diagnosis. The same silence that Heidi had brought me back from. But leaving the way I did might not have been the right reaction either.

My hand moved to cover my mouth as my elbow rested on the door panel. Keeping my focus on the road in front of me, my mind spun with too many emotions and unanswered questions, tearing at my insides. Each of Heidi's questions and accusatory glares burned like salt being rubbed in each of the wounds. If there was a connection between my dream and my childhood, I had yet to discover it. I wasn't positive they were related, but it was a hunch I had been exploring over the past week.

I took a page from Heidi's book and searched high and low for any state news article, public arrest records, or obituary that involved domestic violence over the last twenty years. I assumed domestic violence based the sounds and setting of my dream, but I had no way of knowing if I was remotely close or not. My searches revealed nothing.

My thoughts wondered back to Heidi. She had Connected with me. She had been there enduring every heart-pounding encounter with me. I shuddered as my blood ran cold. This wasn't her burden to bear. I wanted to understand it first in case I needed to protect her from the truth. A thought occurred to me – Did I chose not to see her? Did I chose not to acknowledge her help?

*Is that what I was doing now?*

I shook my head, throwing the doubt away. I knew better. I didn't need to have my full memory to know that danger lurked behind the veil barely separating me from the truth. I didn't want her anywhere near it, getting sucked into whatever ugly awaited me.

But she was right. Nothing would have stopped me from going with her that night, to confront that delusional doctor, to protect her from whatever ugliness that awaited her.

But this was different.

Wasn't it?

I drove, allowing myself to get lost in my thoughts, until my eye lids became heavy. Every minute on the highway was spent weighing my options. How could I learn the truth that I deserved to know without pushing Heidi further away?

My time was up, my eyelids growing heavier with exhaustion, I pulled into a rest stop. I would take a quick nap then turn around and go home to fix things with her. If I was going to fully commit to Heidi, I had to do it the right way. I had to let my walls down.

# Chapter 15

## Heidi

When I woke up this morning, Duncan's side of the bed was empty and cold. I shuffled to the living room, hoping to see him asleep on the couch, but it was empty too. Peeking through the living room window, his truck wasn't in the driveway either. He hadn't come home. I had no messages or missed calls either.

My heart sank to my stomach and my chest ached as realization struck me. I'd be doing this alone today – my first prenatal appointment.

The drive to Easton City was spent pushing down my thoughts. I didn't want to be sad on a day that was supposed to be joyous. After checking in, I was asked to leave a urine sample in the bathroom before taking a seat. It felt so strange to pee in a tiny cup, I was so nervous I thought I might miss it. Thankfully I hadn't.

I now sat anxiously in the waiting room of the doctor's office. The pictures of babies in various poses against different backdrops and scenes were likely meant to bring joy. But for me, it only brought uncertainty. The drunk little grins on their faces knew of no heartbreak. I wasn't sure that my baby would have the same luxury.

The little voice in my head that was clearly Team Duncan replayed over and over in my thoughts. *The decisions he makes are intentional. He cares for his things. Trust him.*

While the voice that no longer wanted to play the fool rebutted. *If there's a reason, why hasn't he told me? Why doesn't he trust you enough to let you truly see him?*

My thoughts turned to assumptions, then to anger, and finally to sorrow, flinging me around the mental arena of my mind. *Get. A. Grip.* Olivia's voice rang as a reminder in my warring thoughts.

I could make one of two choices: let Duncan walk away from us, and move on with my life, or, fight for him. Fight for the love that I knew he was capable of offering. Fight for the life that I had always wanted. Fight for the father of my child to remain in our lives and get our happily ever after.

"Heidi Miller," a voice called from the front of the room. My head snaped up, shifting my vision from the floor to the tall woman in lavender scrubs holding a manila-colored file folder. Her curious glance spilled over me as I remained seated.

"Oh, right. That's me." I grabbed my purse, slid its strap over my shoulder, and joined her at the front of the waiting room.

She turned on her heels, peering down at the contents of her hands, and walked briskly down the hall she had come from, flicking her head for me to follow her. "Date of birth?"

"Seven, seven, ninety-six.

We came to a halt, and she extended her arm into the opened doorway of the exam room. I entered and sat my purse down on the seat of the empty chair in the corner of the room. The chair that Duncan should have been sitting in right now.

Worry started to creep its way back up my throat

when a slam brought me back to attention. The nurse had shut the door and was busy laying various items out on the counter. A white paper drape, gloves, two packaged towelettes and a panty liner. She faced me with a gentle yet worn expression, ready to instruct me. "Go ahead and get undressed from the waist down. Drape this sheet across your waist and take a seat on the table for me. The doctor will be in shortly." She offered a swift hollow smile before exiting the room, shutting the door behind her.

I complied and sat my naked butt on the white paper that lined the exam table. The crinkle echoed in the empty room, reminding me again that I was alone. And I really wished I wasn't.

About ten minutes later, a knock sounded on the door of the exam room before it opened slightly, and Dr. Lauren Mathis asked if she was able to enter. Dr. Mathis was a woman in her mid to late fifties if I had to guess. She had a few gray hairs near her temples which were brushed back into a knot of hair contained by a large claw clip. Her smile lines were deep and beautifully worn. Her smile reached her bright blue eyes as she extended her hand to me. "I'm Dr. Lauren Mathis, it's nice to meet you."

I shook her hand and said, "Nice to meet you too."

She rolled the round green pleather stool from the counter to the end of the exam table in front of me. I was suddenly conscious that the only thing that covered my lady parts was a thin white paper sheet. I had to fight the awkwardness of the thought. "So today we're here to confirm your pregnancy. We'll check your pelvic area, ensure your reproductive organs look healthy, then we'll capture some measurements if a gestational sac is found."

I nodded along, concentrating on her words like I knew exactly what she was talking about. I didn't. A quick tap tap on the door sounded before it opened wide. I watched as the nurse in the lavender scrubs rolled in a piece of equipment with a monitor, an odd shaped keyboard, and some sort of wand looking device handing from the side. She shut the door behind her and lined up the machine next to the exam table.

Dr. Mathis pulled two stirrups from somewhere inside the frame of the table and pulled them up. She taped each one, "Go ahead and place your heels here and lie back." I did as she said. She pulled the machine closer towards her and made a few clicks on the keys. "Go ahead and scootch your butt to the edge of the table for me please." She took a seat on the stool between my spread knees. The sheet trying it's damnedest to protect me from the awkward exposure. The doctor pulled a pair of gloves over her hands and the lavender clad nurse pulled a condom over the wand before swirling a dollop of some sort of jelly on top before handing it to the doctor.

"The lube will be a little cold and you'll feel a little pressure, but it shouldn't hurt. If it does, please let me know." I nodded and swallowed hard.

I *really* wished Duncan was here with me. Or Olivia.

Dr. Mathis pushed the sheet up over my knees, exposing me as discreetly as she could while making sure she could line the wand up with my opening. "A little pressure," she reminded me as she gently pushed the wand inside me.

The sensation was odd and foreign. I could feel my body tensing around it, hindering an easy entry. The doctor asked if I was okay. I nodded, took a breath and tried to relax. I decided to focus on the screen of black and white wavy lines next to me. Distorted shapes curved and bowed across the screen as the wand twisted and pushed inside me, probing the nausea back to life.

The doctor used her free hand to press a combination of buttons and key to capture images of what she explained were my uterus and ovaries. She prodded my insides with the wand a few more times, stabbing my organs looking for something. She held the wand still and made a few more clicks on the keyboard.

A fast, whooshing sound came to life next to me. She turned the screen towards me for a better view and pointed to a tiny bean shape on the screen. "Your baby's heartbeat is strong." Her words were carried by her elated smile. Even the nurse's smile carried genuine delight. "You're measuring at eight weeks and two days."

A strip of pictures of the black and white lines printed from the front of the machine. Finally, the wand was being withdrawn from me and the white sheet was pulled back down to cover me. "You can sit back up if you'd like," the nurse said as she pulled the pictures from the machine and handed them to me.

The doctor removed her gloves and washed her hands before turning back to me. "Feel free to take your time to clean yourself up. The bathroom is down the hall to the left if you need it. Once you finish up, please take a seat back in the lobby and someone will call you back to complete a few labs. You'll be able to schedule your next appointment at that time too. Then you'll be free to go."

We exchanged pleasantries before I was left alone in the room once again. I jumped down off the table and felt the goop leak from inside me. I crossed my legs, to prevent it from sliding further down my thighs. I seethed inwardly, not just at Duncan for leaving me like he did, but also at myself for not just telling him sooner. I shouldn't have to be here alone. This was by far the most invasive and uncomfortable situation I've ever been in, and I was pissed, and hurt, that I was here by myself.

I cleaned myself up and had just buttoned my jeans when my phone buzzed inside my purse. I dug through its contents, careful not to damage the ultrasound photos I had placed inside. My heart raced with hope and anticipation as I found my phone. I was desperate to hear Duncan's voice and didn't pay attention to the name that flashed across the screen before answering. "Duncan?"

"Heidi. It's Detective Reid. We need to talk."

# Chapter 16

## Heidi

I could barely contain my angst as I sat for blood work back at the doctor's office. The nurse assumed I had a needle phobia. She kept instructing me to take deep breaths and not to look at the needle or the tubes that quickly filled with my blood.

But no, I was too busy trying to decode Detective Ried's tone. Was he suspicious? Curious? I couldn't tell. The gruff in his voice left no room for an accurate assumption of his objective.

He asked that I meet him at my apartment. "My apartment?" I asked confused.

"I could hear him shuffle through some papers. "Yes. Your apartment at the corner of First and Burlington Avenue. Apartment 505."

"Where'd you get that address?"

"Your employer," his tone etched my ears with frustration. "Is this not your correct address? Dr. Graham advised this was your address in the city. Do I need to meet you at your Mount Hopewell residence? Or better yet, you could just meet me at the police station."

"No, my city address is fine." My skin felt molten. How dare Graham make such an assumption. I made a mental note to confront him about it later. I was in no mood for bullshit today. I would have much rather preferred to meet at my own house, but I was already in the city. I told him I was finishing up with a doctor's appointment then I would be there. He seemed to be mildly content with my response and hung up with a grunt.

Finally, making my way inside the apartment building, I was once again taken aback by the sleek and contemporary features. The cool air rushed around me as I strode across the gray veined marbled floor to the elevators. I pressed the button for the fifth floor, swallowing the many emotions trying to rise in my throat.

Graham texted me almost immediately after Detective Reid hung up earlier. 'The key is under the mat. It's your copy to keep.' I scoffed, tossing the phone in my purse.

And now, here I was, getting off the elevator that led me to apartment 505. At my feet, a welcome mat that read 'Home Sweet Home' hid the key waiting for me. I rolled my eyes, ignoring the message. Retrieving the key and sliding it in the door's lock, my eyes went wide with the vision in front of me.

This apartment had the same layout as Graham's above me but was decorated with feminine undertones. A large silvery gray plush couch sat in the middle of the living room, overlooking the stunning view of downtown. Matching armchairs sat on either side, facing parallel to the expansive window. Against the back wall, on the opposite side of the apartment was a floor to ceiling bookshelf. Not many books resided on its shelves, but intricate vases and small semi erotic statues did. Warm vanilla scents wafted thought the air from the diffuser that sat on the table behind the couch.

The sterile white walls were accented with

wainscoting moulding and dotted with enlarged images I was sure Mr. Keller captured.

Graham's dad stepped away from his career as a medical researcher and took up his hobby full time. This allowed him to be present in Graham's life since his own mom, Dr. Keller, didn't appear to have any desire to participate in the day-to-day requirements of being a parent.

These pictures, much like the ones that hung at the Keller Institute, captured life from an unique perspective. However, unlike the pictures at the institute, these pictures were intimate and titillating. The first image that caught my attention was of two hands. A small, female hand with her palm pressed into the mattress was covered by a much larger male's hand. His fingers interlaced with hers as the sinful red sheets bunched around their hands from the pressure of being pushed into the mattress beneath them.

Another was a black and white image of the side silhouette of a woman lying on the floor with her back arched, her head turned opposite of the camera. Silk draped strategically over her naked and voluptuous curves.

I didn't get a chance to look the other two photos or spend much time studying the unexpected sensations that started to prick between my thighs before I heavy thud pounded on the door, causing my heart to do the same. I battled the blush that built while I was looking at the pictures.

I rushed to answer the door. Stunned to see Detective Ried's tall, yet doughy figure. His figure was punctuated with a round middle and wrinkles permanently set in his forehead, no doubt from carrying that grumpy scowl. Gray hair covered his head, and his lips were pressed in a thin line. "Hello, Detective. Please come in." His presence made me jumpy. His gray eyes were cold and unreadable.

He entered the threshold of the apartment and did a quick survey of the space around him as I shut the door behind him. He flicked his eyes between each sensual piece of artwork that inhabited the living room then to me. "So, this isn't your primary address I take it."

I blew a breath, thankful that it was obvious that this wasn't my choice of style, but quickly regained composure when I realized his gray eyes stared suspiciously at me. "No, sir."

I scrambled to think of something that would lighten the suspicion. "Graham offered this space to me if I were ever to need it while I was here in the city. Since my primary residence is a two-hour drive from here, there may be times where I should stay closer to the institute. For the benefit of my patients," I rationalized.

He nodded curtly and took a seat at one of the barstools at the kitchen counter. He held his hand gesturing towards the one next to him. I planted myself in it. "I'll get straight to the point," he folded his arms across his chest, and rested them on his gut. "There's not many people back at the station who are buying this 'I found out in a dream' story you and Dr. Graham have been spinning."

It was hard to keep the shock from my expression. I knew that could be a possibility, but now that it was in my face, I was unprepared with untrained emotions. I swallowed hard, "I know how it sounds. Believe me. It was hard enough to explain it to my family too. And I'm not sure my mom is convinced. My dad has been supportive though…" I was babbling under his no nonsense glare. "…but I can prove it."

Detective Reid held his stare, blank intensity, pushing me to continue my explanation.

"Earlier this month, I helped located a lost birdwatcher. His name is Michael."

Detective Reid took out his pen and started to take notes. "Does this Michael have a last name?"

*Shit.* "Yes…but I don't remember it."

His pen went back to the paper.

"But he and the rest of the group stayed at the Antlers Lodge in Mount Hopewell. You could get his name from the visitor's log."

"Okay. And how did you locate him?"

"Through my dream." I went on to explain every detail of my dream and how we found Michael exactly where he said he was. I also explained that in my dream, Michael told me what happened and how he wound up lost and injured. When I visited him in the hospital, he relayed the same details to me as he had previously. "And, if you're inclined, I could try and Connect with you too." It was bold of me to offer, but I worried that he wouldn't take Michael's word since he was unconscious during his rescue. With everything going on right now, I didn't want the weight of police suspicion added to my already full plate.

Detective Reid considered my proposal. "How would that work?"

"Well, I'm still trying to figure that out," his grumpy scowl returned. "But Graham and I together might be able to find you and Connect with you quicker. If we're both looking for you, our chances at a Connection will be more successful."

His posture squared and he leaned a little closer into my space. "I'm going to give the two of you just this one opportunity to…" his eyes looked back over the note pad he used to scribe our interaction on, "Connect with me. If it turns out you're both full of shit, I will personally haul the two of you in myself." His tone was heavy with his promise.

My body shuddered at the thought of sitting in a cold jail cell. Could he really do that when we were innocent?

As if he could hear my thoughts himself, he said, "There's no evidence to support that the two of you didn't conspire with Dr. Keller to commit her crimes." My mouth fell open at his comment. "And the two of you sure know an awful lot about crimes that neither of you committed." He used air quotes around the word 'committed'. He stood from his stool and stalked towards the door, looking over his shoulder back at me. "I expect you to stay local until your claims can be corroborated."

The door closed behind him as he left, taking all the air inside the apartment with its pull.

Fear and frustration built in my gut; this was not something I thought I'd have to worry about today. Connecting with Detective Reid had become my number one priority at the moment. Immediately, I retrieved my phone, and my thumbs ran feverishly over the screen as I sent the following text – I need you.

# Chapter 17

## Heidi

"Everything will be okay. We will find him."

I paced in front of the couch, letting my gaze get lost in the movement of downtown instead of letting my eyes settle on his handsome features. "How do you know that, Graham?" Panic had fully set it as soon as Detective Reid left. If Graham and I couldn't Connect with him, and prove our ability to be true, we would be arrested for whatever crimes he thought we committed with Dr. Keller.

"Because, if anyone can…"

I eyed him, "I'm not interested in your empty platitudes." My hands instinctively wrapped around my belly. A father who may not want us and mother stuck in a jail cell for crimes she couldn't even fathom to commit. *Look at me, well on my way to being mother of the year.* I was going to be sick.

I felt Graham's strong arm wrap around me and pull me into his hard chest. My arms still wrapped around my belly, my head fell, exhausted, against his chest. Both of his arms were wrapped around me now and he swayed me gently side to side, rubbing one of his hands against my back as his other one held me securely to him.

We stayed like that for several minutes, watching the sun sit low in the sky as evening approached. Each pass of his hand over my back removed a little more of the panic and eventually I felt confident. I lifted my head and offered a half smile of gratitude.

"Heidi," his silky tone caressed my name, causing my breaths to falter. "I'm confident that we will be able to Connect with Detective Ried tonight. It's not just my opinion, but the science also proves it. I'm not sure you fully grasp the significance of your EEG readings. Your ability is unprecedented, not just because of its rarity, but because of your strength. Your ability to follow a Connection surpasses my own." His hand cusped my cheek, stroking it gently with his thumb. "I don't think you understand how special you really are."

Graham's lips were just a breath away from mine now. A familiar intensity made my mouth go dry. "Graham," I nearly croaked out, and pressed my hands against his chest trying to create space from us. But he didn't budge. I stepped one foot out behind me to remove myself from his orbit. "I appreciate your confidence in me. But this has to work. We have to do whatever we can to make sure our Connection is successful. I don't understand how you're not more worried about this right now?"

Graham was a vision of calm and he returned to his seat on the couch. He leaned back, laid his arms out on the back of the couch of either side of him and crossed one ankle over his knee. "Heidi, we're innocent. Not even a hell-bent detective could uncover any evidence that remotely ties us to any crimes committed by my mother. Any competent lawyer could argue that point."

"A lawyer?" I dragged my hands down my face and resumed my pacing. "I can't afford a lawyer."

"Listen, let's take this one step at a time, okay?" I

felt his consuming brown eyes watch me as I paced back and forth. "Tonight, the goal is to Connect. That's it."

"And what if it doesn't work?"

"Then it'll be tomorrow's problem. But you working yourself up right now won't help either of our chances tonight."

Defeated, I plopped down on the opposite end of the couch. I knew he was right, but dammit, this was the last thing I wanted to worry about right now. "Okay," I huffed. "What's our plan?"

*** 

After a quick supper of Chinese takeout while we discussed the plan for tonight, Graham ran upstairs to retrieve a few things for my stay tonight. I took the opportunity to call Olivia. She wasn't thrilled with the idea of me staying in the city until Detective Reid was satisfied with our explanation but there was no getting around the law. I gave her the address of where I was staying just in case she needed it. Trying to lighten the mood, she tried asking how excited Duncan was to find out he was going to be a father. I couldn't bring myself to tell her that I hadn't told him. Or that he walked out last night, and I hadn't heard from him since. If I wasn't still so angry, I'd be worried about him. But until I figured out how to handle the situation, I decided I couldn't waste any emotion on him that he wasn't willing to waste on me.

It felt juvenile but I didn't know what else to do in the moment. My phone chirped quickly in my ear, alerting me that my battery was about to die at any second. Which was fine. Any longer on the phone with my sister and she would have seen right through my poor attempt to make everything sound like rainbows and sunshine.

"Call me in the morning with an update," she asked.

"I promise. Goodnight."

"Night. Love ya."

"Love you too."

I sat my phone down on the arm of the couch just in time for it to buzz its final buzz. I reached for my purse that sat on the floor next to where I sat on the couch. I unfolded the ultrasound pictures of my little bean. I didn't know yet if it was a boy or a girl, I wouldn't know for a while, but its little life flashed before my eyes. Its first smile. First steps. First day of school. Learning to ride a bike.

Would Duncan decide to be a part of it all?

The door of the apartment opened, startling me, causing me to quickly and carefully fold the pictures back up and return them to my purse.

"I found a spare charger and brought you something to sleep in." Graham sat the pile of clothes and charger on the counter in the kitchen before making his way deeper inside the apartment. "The bed in the last room on the left is made up with clean sheets and there's fresh towels in the closet in the bathroom. Also, if you look in the drawer under the sink, you'll find new toothbrushes."

Among all the chaos, I forgot to ask him earlier. "Graham, why do you have this place?" I stood to meet his gaze. "And what's with these pictures? This entire place feels like it's powered by sexual tension."

He shot me a wicked smirk, "So, you feel it too?"

"What? No." I tucked my hair behind my ear. "That's not what I meant."

He chuckled at my flustered attempt to deflect. He stalked towards me with his palms flipped up and held them in front of him, as if he was offering up a sacrifice. "This is my studio."

"Your studio?"

He pointed to the hung photos. "These are mine. I took these." His eyes flashed with pride. "You asked me before if I took up an interested in photography too…"

"And you said no."

"I said I tried. It never caught on for me like it had for my father. He could point his lens at anything and capture its beauty. But me, I didn't have an eye to find the beauty in ordinary things. Only the extraordinary." His gaze intensified as his eyes drank me in, completely helpless against the effect he had on me. I hated it.

"So…is this some sort of porn studio then?"

His sultry laugh reached my ears, bringing goosebumps with it. "Here, let me show you." He turned towards the first hallway on his left and I hesitantly followed him. My mouth fell agape once I saw what was behind the door. A four-poster king sized bed with red satin sheets and sheer black drapes gathered at each of its corners was the main focus. There were tripods, cameras, and lighting equipment posted strategically around the large room. In one of the corners, a wide body length mirror rested in the corner. Several pieces of silks and satins sat folded in a basket next to the door. There was also a chest further down that same wall that I didn't dare ask what was inside. "I take boudoir photos for women, and couples, who want to boost their sexual confidence." My mouth still open, he used his hand to tenderly cup my jaw and close it. "That's why I have the living area decorated the way it is. The images and sculptures elicit a primal and sensual response that naturally makes my clients feel comfortable and confident from the start of our session."

Tara's words came back to me. The conversations she had overheard from the hall outside his office when she thought he was cheating on his girlfriend at the time. He wasn't cheating or sleeping around, he was booking clients. Maybe he wasn't as morally gray as I thought. I stepped into the room, running my fingers over the luxurious satin sheets before taking a seat on the edge of the mattress. Looking around at the equipment and props, I still didn't understand why he said the apartment was available if I needed it. "Why did you give Detective Reid this address?" I asked.

His eyebrow arched in response as he leaned against the doorway, staring at me curiously.

"Reid, when he asked you for my address, why did you give him this one?"

"Ah." He pushed away from the door frame with his shoulder and sat next to me. "I gave him both of your addresses."

"But this isn't my place. Why not just give him my actual address?"

"Because I meant what I said. This place is yours if you want it. If you need it."

"What about your studio?"

"I can find a new one."

"Oh, you'll just find a new one?" I asked with a droll stare.

Graham chuckled softly, "Yes." He leaned in closer to me, tucking a strand of hair behind my ear, staring at me with amused and hungry eyes. "If you stayed here, I would find a new studio. There's nothing that I wouldn't do for you, Heidi. All you have to do is ask."

# Chapter 18

## Duncan

My tires angrily kicked up gravel as I backed out of Ronny's driveway and tore thought the streets and highways towards Easton City. My knuckles turned white from my grip on the steering well.

After I stormed out on Heidi last night, I had to pull over and sleep. I drove for hours before finally having to stop. I slept way too long and by the time I woke up, I was already an hour late for work. It took me about two hours to get home. When I got back to my house to freshen up, Heidi was already gone. Which I suspected since she usually left for work around seven. Not wanting eavesdropping ears to overhear us, I didn't go to the store to apologize. I acted like a fucking idiot last night and planned on making it up to her.

I spent all day trying to think of a way to apologize to her. Typing and deleting then retyping words in a message to her. I ultimately decided a text wasn't the appropriate way to ask for forgiveness. Instead, I decided I'd show up at her place with groceries and cook her a romantic dinner. I was sure to grab two bottles of red wine and ice cream from my pantry and freezer before I left. But when I got to her house her car was gone.

I was sure the store was dark and locked up when I drove by it. I called Heidi's cell. Straight to voicemail. I peeled out of her driveway and headed to

Ronny's, certain Olivia would be there. If anyone knew where Heidi was, it would be her sister.

"What do you mean 'Where's Heidi'? Did something happen?"

"That's why I'm here, Olivia." I couldn't keep the panic out of my voice. The last time she went missing, she was basically in a fucking coma. And lying next to that tool, Graham. I seethed inwardly at the memory.

"When I talked to her earlier, she said she was still in Easton City. Did something happen?" Olivia was now panicked and had picked up her phone to call her sister. It went straight to voicemail for her too.

"Wait," I pinched the bridge of my nose. "What do you mean *still* in Easton City?"

Olivia cocked her head and eyebrow, "For her ap…" Her moth shut abruptly. Her eyes widened with a realization, and she refused to enlighten me.

"Why is she in Easton City? She hadn't mentioned she needed to go into the institute this week."

She just held her hands up and shook her head. "It's not for me to say, Duncan. I'm sorry."

I knew she was, and I didn't want to press too hard if she was following her sisterly code. I just needed to know that Heidi was okay. "Is there anything you can tell me?"

She sighed and pulled a piece of paper from her pants pocket. "She's at this address."

I swallowed hard and tried to steady my hands as my heart shattered. Rage and fear ignited inside of me like I had never felt before. I knew this address.

"Duncan, calm down bro. If you're thinking of doing anything rash let's stop and talk about it for a second," my brother tried to reason with me.

My eyes snapped to him, "And if it was Olivia? What would you do? Hm?"

I waited for Ronny to come up with a reason that was good enough not to go after the woman of his dreams. But one never came, all he said was, "Give him hell."

"Exactly."

"She can't leave!" Olivia yell behind me.

I didn't stop and ask for an explanation as I tore through the door and back to my truck without a goodbye or thanks. I needed to go get my girl.

It was nearing seven o'clock and I was itching to get out of my truck and give Graham a piece of my mind, and fist. Then I was getting my woman and getting the fuck out of there. And praying like hell she'd forgive me.

Again.

# Chapter 19

## Heidi

After the day I've had, I was ready to shower and wash the day away.

Graham called Eric and informed him I wouldn't be able to Connect with him tonight but gave him some skills to work on in the meantime. He also called Detective Reid and explained some basic techniques to him to help him experience a lucid dream. He also gave him some items to think of while going to sleep in hopes it would help us identify his Connection quicker. We didn't want to waste time chasing Connections and risk Detective Reid waking up before we've had the opportunity to find him.

Even if we were able to Connect with him, it didn't mean he would remember or be able to interact with us.

Graham and I spend more time going over the plan to identify the most Connections as possible. This wasn't something we had tried before but felt we might as well give it a shot.

We planned to split up, each taking a different Connection until we found Detective Ried's. Once we found it, we'd somehow have to signal to the other to meet them there. This was the part that would be completely new territory for us. But we were hopeful it could work. I've been able to follow him, and he's been able to follow me into other Connections in the past, we'd just need to make sure our calls were intentional and pay attention to them.

Finally showered, having the stress of the day washed away, I slipped into the heather gray tee shirt Graham let me borrow. It was more slender than Duncan's shirts, but the length was about the same. It was just long enough to cover my ass.

The pants however, kept sliding down. The draw string couldn't be pulled tight enough and no matter how many times I rolled the waist down, they still slid. I opted to go pants-less. It's not like he'll be down here for much longer anyway. We're going to go over our plan one more time before we went to bed. In our respective apartments.

I exited the bathroom and found Graham sitting at the kitchen counter, shirtless, reviewing the notes I had written down in the notebook earlier in the evening. I approached the empty barstool beside him and took a seat. "You're shirtless. Aren't you cold?"

His eyebrow arched as he lazily dragged his eyes down my body. "You're pants-less. Aren't *you* cold?"

*Touche.*

"So," I twisted my tangled brunette waves together and tossed the giant strand over my shoulder for it to lay in the center of my back. "Think this will work, our calls to each other?"

"I do."

A heavy knock pounded at the door, causing me to jump and look warily at Graham. "Think Detective Reid changed his mind about tonight?"

Graham was already up and approaching the door. He ducked his head down to the peep hole. He shot me a look, irked by whoever was pounding on the door. He swung the door opened, blocking my view of whoever stood at the door.

Before I could even ask who it was, Graham was stumbling backwards into the apartment, holding his jaw.

I jumped off my stool, unsure if should run or stay. Graham recovered quickly and charged the opened doorway. I heard that distinct snap of skin-to-skin contact then some shuffling of weight being thrown around in the corridor between the door and elevator. I poked my head around the door to get a glimpse of the commotion.

"Duncan!" My voice a surprised shrill. I wanted to make my way to the pounds of flesh that were throwing elbows and fists at each other, but I feared I would get pulled into the vortex of idiocy.

"Graham!" I tried to get his attention too but neither of them heard me over the blows being delivered. I hollered for them again, but still, no response. So, I did the only thing I could think of to get a man's attention. I flashed them.

"Hey!" I pulled the hem of my shirt up, revealing my bare breasts. The sudden exposure to the chill in the corridor made my nipples harden against it.

Their attention shot to me and my nearly bare body. I smirked proudly; I had their attention now. Green and brown eyes became entranced by the sight of my tits. Satisfied that they wouldn't resume their pissing contest, I released my shirt, letting the fabric fall down the front of my body.

"Now, if we're all ready to act like adults, lets dust ourselves off, and get inside." I took a few steps backwards, making sure not to break eye contact with them, to step fully inside the apartment again.

Graham and Duncan, both slightly haggard, had little cuts littering each of their faces. It looked like Graham was already developing a massive bruise under his right eye though. They nodded a momentarily truce and both tried to shove through the door at the same time. I rolled my eyes and pointed to the couch in the living room. Begrudgingly they both complied, and I shut the door before following them to the living room.

If looks could kill, I'd have two fine ass men dead at my feet. I cleared my throat as I stood in front of them, commanding their attention again, only this time, I left the girls where they belonged.

Duncan eyed my bare legs before shooting me a look that bordered on accusatory.

"Don't start with me, Duncan. After the shit you pulled last night, you've got no room to make any judgments." I looked between the both of them, waiting for one of them to start explaining. But they both sat silently, only making my blood boil with angry annoyance. "Will someone please tell me what the hell is going on?"

Graham shrugged and rubbed his jaw, "Ask your fucking boyfriend. He's the one who showed up swinging."

I looked expectantly at Duncan. "Well?"

"I came here to get you. To take you home."

I scoffed. "If you wanted me home, you would've stayed while I was there."

"Damn man, what'd you do? She's pissed." Duncan shot him a glare and growled, "Mind your fucking business, prick."

"You're in *my* apartment. This *is* my business."

"This might be *your* apartment, but that's is *my* girlfriend."

"Not for long if you keep pulling your shit."

Duncan shot to his feet, rage fuelling him, "Is that a threat?"

"Enough! So help me, God, if I have to get butt ass naked to get any sense of accession over you two, I will." I saw something dark glint across Graham's eyes as he relaxed back into that calm demeaner he displayed earlier today. Duncan sat his ass down with a quickness and didn't dare utter another word.

"Duncan, I'm sorry you came all this way, but now isn't a good time. Graham and I are in the middle of trying to save our asses." His mouth parted as to interject but I cut him off. "And moreover, I'm still too pissed to even look at you right now."

Hurt and betrayal stretched across his handsome face. I tried to bite my tongue, but the words slipped out before I could stop them. "It doesn't feel good, does it? Feeling like you have a shot at everything you've ever wanted, just to have the wool pulled over your eyes. At least I gave you an explanation."

Before I could feel bad for being so harsh, I moved my focus to Graham. "And you. You don't get to walk in here, with your smoulder and lack of boundaries for personal space, offering me 'support' at every turn. I'm a big girl. And I don't *need*, either of you." That faltered Graham's confidence. "Now," I walked towards the door to open it and leaned against it. "If you both could be so kind and get the hell out."

They both shot each other a 'now look what you've done' kind of look and slunk towards the door. Graham stopped just in front of me, leaning a little too close, completely ignoring my warning from earlier. "I'll see you tonight. I'll be there when you call for me. You've got this." He winked at me before casually tossing his glance over his shoulder at Duncan, walking out into the corridor.

I felt Duncan's chest rumble as he growled towards Graham and encapsulated me between his thick arms, chest, and the door. My heart raced with anticipation as a mix of senses trampled across my body.

His earthy scent filled my nostrils. The heave of his chest just barely brushing against my nipples as it rose and fell. I was nearly coming undone beneath his intense green gaze.

No one owned my pleasure like he did. He wanted Graham to know it and I didn't want to stop him.

He dropped his mouth to my ear, pausing to nuzzle my hair, taking in my own scent, before his heady voice filled my ear. "Do what you need to do tonight. But tomorrow, I'm taking you home."

And if I wasn't being tortured enough, he slid his knee between my thighs, applying pressure to my swollen center. I squeezed my eyes and inner muscles, trying to ignore the orgasm that was defiantly building inside me.

I felt Duncan smirk against my ear, "Ready?"

My eyes popped opened. *Ready for what?*

His left arm snaked around me, sliding my hips forward up his thigh, rewarding me with the most delicious friction. A storm of ecstasy was released. A typhoon exploding between my thighs. My arms anchored around his neck as my head fell back, hitting the door from the force of my release.

He growled, low and gratifyingly in my ear. No words were needed. He was laying claim to what was his.

Gently releasing me, he removed himself from where he hovered over me and entered the corridor.

I couldn't bear to look in their direction once Duncan joined Graham. I blamed this stupid sex apartment for charging me up the way I was. I had enough of both of them and slammed the door in their face.

I had shit to do.

# Chapter 20

## Duncan

Even though she slammed the door in our face, I took this as victory.

She allowed herself to come undone for me, and in front of Graham. Stepping inside the elevator, I pressed the button for the sixth floor. Graham shot me a questioning look. "Nothing. Just making sure you get home safely."

Graham snorted.

"Is something funny?" I snarled.

His expression twisted with amusement. "You're a real class act, you know that?" He shook his head. "Do you even know what you have, man?"

I did. *Didn't I?*

"Because I do. And you bet your ass I'm going to be there for her when you fuck up and fail her for the last time. When she realizes I can provide her with everything you can't, I'll be there."

My patience and civility were becoming non-existent around this guy. The elevator finally dinged, signalling our arrival. It took everything I had not to spartan kick his ass right out of this elevator.

Instead, I held the door opened after he exited, "If you insist." I glanced down at my thigh, where my jeans were damp from Heidi's release, then back to him. "I hope you enjoy the show."

His expression piqued, I removed my hand from the elevator's opening and stood in the center.

"How'd you like your preview?"

His eyes grew almost black as the elevator doors closed, removing him from my sight and mind. Now I was free to get what I came for.

The elevator ride back down to the next floor took excruciatingly long. I could feel the veins throbbing in my neck, pressure budding at the root of my shaft. The elevator chimed once more, and I willed the doors to open faster.

Blood shot to the tip of my cock once I saw her. Her expression was a mix between anger and lust.

"Duncan," one hand on her hip and the other held a pointed finger, ready to scold me "I need…"

She never stood a chance. I swallowed her reproval with my kiss as I leaned down to scoop her under her ass. Wrapping her strong legs around me. I pushed her into the door and trailed my kisses from her mouth to her neck, feeling my dick twitch with every moan she rewarded me with.

Once inside the apartment and the door closed, I slid her down my body and pulled my shirt off over my head. Her eyes lingered on my chest before I saw the cogs start turning in her mind. "Duncan, we need to talk."

I stepped to her, cupping the sides of her face, bring her lips to mine. My kiss was hard and predatory. I scooped her up again and walked further into the living room with her.

"Duncan," she breathed, as I released her from another kiss. "It's. Important."

I punctuated each word with a kiss, desperately trying to calm her mind.

Her head rolled to the side after the last one,

exposing her neck perfectly for me. I kissed, nipped, and licked the sensitive skin from her chin to her collar bone. I could feel her core soaking the bare skin of my stomach. I needed to feel her.

Towards the end of the apartment, down one of the halls, I saw the illumination of a dim light. I followed it, hoping it would lead me to a bedroom.

It did.

Heidi's hips undulated against me, whimpering with pleasure and mumbling something. I didn't bother to shut the door as I laid her on the middle of the bed. I nipped her chin before leaving a trail of kisses over her shirt, between her breast, down her stomach, and finally to her mound.

I took a moment to revel in her scent before rolling the end of the tee shirt to above her breasts. My eyes dragged lazily between each one before images rushed back to me.

Heidi, standing in the hallway, tits out, Graham looking a little too hard for my liking. I dipped my head and lowered my mouth over a stiff nipple, flicking my tongue roughly against it. Her head pushed further into the mattress as her chest arched upward. I moved my head to the other one, but before I pulled her nipple into my mouth, I cursed myself for asking the question, but I had to know. "Was that the first time?"

"The first time what?" Her words came out in pants, her hands clawing at my arms, trying to pull me back in.

"Him," I growled, eyeing her up and down, "seeing you like this."

She took a second to register my question before

shaking her head. "He's never seen me this exposed."
I took note of how she answered the question and had
full intention on following up on it later. But for now,
we both needed this release.

I rewarded her with pulling her nipple between
my teeth, flicking my tongue across it. She hissed
with satisfaction.

I tucked my hand inside her panties, palming her
wet center. *Fuuuuuck.* I slid my middle finger
between her slippery folds, dragging it up and down,
ensuring to apply the slightest pressure to her clit.

"Duncan, wait. Please."

I stilled, but she didn't say anything more. She
just stared deep into my eyes. The golden flecks of
her eyes shone brighter that I'd seen in a while. The
love she carried for me, I could see it now in her gaze.
I stood, never letting my eyes leave hers, as I
undressed myself completely.

"Do you want me?" I asked as I kneeled back on
the bed, sliding her panties down her legs and placed
one of my knees between her but stopped mid crawl
when she hadn't answered.

Something else flicked in her eye, something I
couldn't make out. If she no longer wanted me, I
needed to hear her say it. "Heidi, will you have me?"

I thought I saw her eyes gloss over before she
blinked away whatever emotion she held there. "Will
you stop running from me?"

I could hear the faintest break in her words. I
studied her expression a bit longer. "Heidi Miller, I
am yours. Forever and always. I promise."

She pulled her shirt over her head and her legs
spread wider for me, "Then yes. The answer is yes." I

hovered over her as she held me with her gaze. "I wanted you then. I want you now. And I want you forever."

Her words melted over me. The love she held for me didn't make sense. For some unfathomable reason, I was the one she wanted.

I lined my deprived dick with her opening and slammed into her with a punishing thrust. "You will have me forever," I declared, punctuating each word with a thrust. "You own my heart. You own my pleasure. You own my future. You own my past."

She wrapped her legs around me, pulling me deeper into her as I continued sliding my length in and out of her slick sex. I couldn't take my eyes of her.

Heidi's eyes rolled shut and I felt her insides squeeze as she tilted her hips down and held me captive. Just like she did our first time. My hips rocked against hers, creating warm friction against her clit.

"Duncan," her whimpers turned to throaty moans. Her hands clawed at the sheets beneath her. The sound of my name, barrelling out of her delicious mouth pushed me to my edge.

I dropped my head to her breast, punishing her nipple with the flick of my tongue while my hand kneaded the other. She threaded her fingers through my hair and gently pulled, bringing my attention to her. Her eyes regarded each scratch and nick that dotted my face.

Holding her gaze with my own, I slowed the roll of my hips against her. Her legs loosened their grip around me, giving me more room to slide out of her.

Pulling out nearly my entire length before gently pushing back inside her. She smiled.

*Fuck me. The hold she had on me was unexplainable.*

I did it again. And again. Increasing the force of my thrust each time until her muscles clenched tight around me. Her eyes rolled shut again, crying out as her release captured my own. I couldn't keep my bellow silent. A primal howl escaped my throat and for the first time in a long time, I felt free.

Figuring out my past was still important; I was just no longer held captive by it. I was no longer alone with it.

I pulled out of her, not caring that our juices spilled onto these luxury sheets, and laid beside her. She was still trying to catch her breath as I slid my hand under hers as it laid resting on her belly.

With a satisfied grin, I asked, "So, what did you need to talk to me about?"

# Chapter 21

## Heidi

"You promise you won't leave?'

He brushed his thumb across mine. "I promise. I'm done running."

I stood from the bed, pulled the grey tee shirt back down over me and retrieved the folded-up pictures from my purse in the living room. He was propped up on one elbow as he waited for my return, and I sat cross-legged on the bed in front of him. I took a steadying breath and handed him the pictures.

He took the photos and unfolded them, viewing all three pictures. He looked confused at first, then a smile grew on his lips that reached his eyes. He leapt from where he was laying on his side, wrapped me in his arms and brought me back down on top of him. He then landed the most tender kiss on my lips. I melted against his body.

"Heidi," Duncan looked up at the pictures in amazement and disbelief. "This is for real. This is our baby?"

I nodded, tears spilling tenderly down my cheeks.

His smile quickly faded with realization. His tone was low and tender. "This is why you were in the city today?" I nodded. "And you went alone?" I nodded again. He placed his forehead against mine and grabbed the back of my neck. "Heidi, I am so unbelievably sorry,"

I shook my head, "Duncan, It's water under the

bridge now. And we can certainly talk more about it later if you'd like but there's a reason why I'm still in the city. I don't have much time to explain." We were well into the night, and I worried that Graham may be looking for me.

He sat, listening intently as I quickly brought him up to speed on Detective Reid's request and how Graham and I were both basically guilty until we could prove our ability. "That's why he was here when you arrived. We've been going over ways to ensure a successful Connection. We've never tried anything like this before, looking for someone that hasn't been involved with the therapy that accompanies a Connection. It's important that you don't wake me in case I still haven't Connected with him."

***

*"Remember what you're looking for?" Graham asked me.*

*"Badges, sirens, a police car, or anything related to your mom's case."*

*"And how are you going to call for me?"*

*"With the basement. You?"*

*"With the store."*

*Graham and I ran down the details one more time before splitting up and chasing Connections independently. We had given Detective Reid some visual cues to focus on as he fell asleep tonight, but there was no guarantee that they would project for us. So, to be on the safe side, we're searching them all. I went first, closing my eyes, trying to focus in on*

Detective Reid. When I opened my eyes again, I was surrounded by cherry blossoms. The trees went on for as far as I could see. "Detective Reid," I called. I walked in a few different directions, searching for him without any luck.

I tried again. Focusing all my might on Reid. But again, when I opened my eyes, there was no sign of him. I attempted a few more Connections before landing in a dream all too familiar.

The same dream that had been plaguing Duncan for a week had started up again. Those same sounds and never-ending hallway built around me, almost everything exactly the same as before. Except, Duncan wasn't an adult, he was a boy. And he was wrapped in the arms of a small blonde girl. She looked to be a little older than Duncan. She was protecting him, but there was no one to protect her.

I didn't know who she was, but maybe Duncan remembered her. As much as it pained me to leave them like this, I had to find Reid.

I put the basement of the Keller Institute in my mind. When I opened my eyes this time, Graham and I were together. "Any luck so far?"

"No."

"Ugh! Maybe he's not sleeping."

"Or maybe we need to wait for a R.E.M cycle. It's likely that he just hasn't started his yet."

And this was why I had to do this with him. I had forgotten all about the simplicity of Connecting from one R.E.M cycle to another. "Okay. We'll hop around a little more and hope that we can find him."

"We could try and find him together." He held out his hand for me to take.

The sooner we found Reid, the sooner I could stop stressing about rotting in a jail cell while I grew a tiny human. I reached out and took his hand. We closed our eyes, focusing on the grumpy detective. I saw a dull and almost overlooked flash. I spoke out loud without opening my eyes. "Graham, did you see that?" The blue light flashed a little brighter this time. "There! Did you see it?"

"Yeah. Let's go."

We opened our eyes to a crime scene. Several Police cars were parked, in various directions along the street with their lights flashing blue and red against the night sky. Yellow crime scene tape tapered off an area of the street and sidewalk. Men and women dressed in blue uniforms moved methodically around the area. I noticed one officer off in the shadows, keeping his distance from the activity unfolding in front of us. I nudged Graham to take a look in that direction.

"You think that's him?" he asked.

I shrugged my shoulders. "Let's go find out."

We approached the young cop, but he barely noticed us until Graham spoke. "Excuse me, sir. What happened here?"

The officer startled but quickly straightened, trying to regain some composure. "This is an active crime scene. You two need to go." He pointed his finger to beyond the barries just on the other side of the intersection. When he did, I was able to get a good look at his badge – 'Reid'. This was it, we found him. Now we could only hope that he remembered when he woke up.

"We did it, Graham. It's him," I said loud enough

*for only Graham to hear.*

*"Told you we would find him." A supporting and friendly smile curled at his lips.*

*"Yes, you did." I held out my hand, "Now let's get going." Being here was making my skin crawl in a sick way.*

*"We should get specifics."*

*"About the scene?" I wasn't sure if I wanted to know.*

*"What if he doesn't remember us? We should get details about the crime scene, that way if this is a lived experience, he'll know we're not full of shit."*

*"And if it's not? What happens if this is just an entirely made-up scenario?"*

*"Then, we'll likely need to lawyer up as a precaution."*

*My shoulder's sagged, and my hand fell back to my side. "All fair points. Let's get this over with."*

*Graham stood straighter, and this time, with more authority in his tone he asked again. "Officer Reid, what happened here?"*

*After a moment of reconciling with his decision, his voice shook when he spoke. "It's awful. Just awful." he swallowed, pushing away the emotion that was building. "A mother and daughter were walking back to their car from the ice cream parlour there." He pointed his glance past Graham to the Scoops & Shakes ice cream shop down the block. "Some idiot driver hopped the curb, struck and killed the mother. The daughter, only thirteen years old, said she hadn't heard the car coming."*

*I scanned the scene once more, the severity finally sinking in. I only noticed then, that in the street near* the curb laid, what was likely the victim, covered by a crimson-stained white sheet. Instinctively, my arms wrapped around my belly, as if I was trying to protect my little bean from the devastation around us.

I felt Graham side eye me before returning his attention to Reid. "Why are you here, and not there helping process the scene?"

Reid's head hung low, "This is my first crime scene." He dragged the back of his hand under his nose before lifting his head up again. "They tell you to keep your composure, not to show emotion, in front of the victims or suspects. But how do I do that when that little girl sitting over there just lost her mother? How do you just accept that you could be eating ice cream one second, then get crushed by a car the next?"

A shudder wracked my body. This version of Reid was riddled with grief. But the Reid I met today was full of suspicion. Was that what happened when you spent your life only seeing the ugly in people?

In the distance, I saw a strike of green. Then yellow. I noticed Graham's attention to it too.

Duncan.

I eyed Graham, worry stretched across my face. Thankfully he was able to read my expression. "I think we have enough to sway him," he said to me.

I took off in the direction of the green and heard Graham say, "Thank you for your time," before his footfalls fell in sync beside me.

The pounds from the pavement beneath our feet turned to a crunch when we Connected. The last time I was here, there was snow everywhere, but now, the ground was blanked by the fallen leaves of Autum.

The greens and yellows bouncing around the dark sky were the only source of light.

In front of us was the house I had seen a little over a week ago. I hadn't spent any time thinking about it lately but here it was again, taunting me like a lost memory.

I listened for the voice I heard last time, but it was complete silence. I slowly scanned the area around the house, trying to convince my feet it was safe to approach. To the left of us, we heard a snap. Graham and I both looked that direction. There, crouched low on the ground, coming around the corner of the front porch was a girl. The only indication from our perspective was her long hair pulled into a low ponytail.

We crouched too, trying to find cover in the shadows of the night as we watched her sneak across the front. Familiarity hit me once she moved closer to the front of the porch. She was the same girl I had seen in Duncan's dream earlier.

Before my brain could fully register, I heard Graham's whisper beside me. "Tawny?"

# Chapter 22

## Heidi

The morning sun and the wight of Duncan's arm around me brought me out of my slumber. I allowed myself to stay safely tucked into him for a few breaths before sneaking away to the kitchen.

I put on a pot of coffee then took a seat at the counter where my notebook still sat. I got busy with noting every Connection I experienced last night. I was sure to highlight the section of the page where I recorded Detective Reid's Connection. I wanted to review it with Graham to make sure I didn't miss anything. We needed to convince Reid that our ability was real. I had only hopped it'd be enough to resolve his suspicions.

Once I was satisfied that I had captured all possible details, I poured myself a cup of coffee. The chocolaty and smoky steam hit my face as I entered the living room and took a seat on the couch. Downtown was already alive and bustling in the morning sun.

My mind circled back to the house and Graham's revelation. Had the girl been Tawny? I was certain, whoever she was, was the same girl I saw hugging and protecting Duncan in his hallway dream. But what made him think she was Tawny?

I searched the corners of my mind for any missed details that could make sense of it all. When none came, I took a sip of the fancy coffee and let the full and slightly bitter taste warm my body with its heat, letting all my thoughts melt with it.

I hadn't realized my eyes were closed or that I had zoned out when I felt the couch dip under the weight of something beside me. A wide hand slid across my belly.

I opened my eyes to see Duncan facing me, sitting sideways with one bent knee on the couch, and the crook of his other knee wresting on top of his ankle. The sunlight glinted across his green eyes as he smiled and stared at my belly, completely ignoring the view in front of us. If I had to guess, it looked like he was imagining what our life looked like as a family. I took another sip of my coffee and tried to remember this moment. Remember this feeling of bliss and hopefulness.

"There's fresh coffee for you if you'd like. I didn't check to see if there was any milk or not."

"Is it decaffeinated?"

I arched my eyebrow at him playfully. "Now why would I put myself through such torture?" I took another sip, making a show of how good it tasted. "The doctor said one cup a day would be okay. So that's what I'll have. Just one cup. And I plan to enjoy every sip."

Duncan, only wearing his boxers I realized, had wondered off to the kitchen for his own cup. I heard the door of the refrigerator open then shut. "No milk, but there's some caramel creamer." I turned to watch him pop the top and take a quick sniff. He winced his head back, "Oof. Not even Mrs. Trudy's chocolate smells this sweet." He eyed the bottle before placing it on the counter. Opening the cabinet above the coffee pot, he pulled down a coffee mug then proceeded to carefully drip the overly sweet elixir into his cup before filling it with coffee and making his way back to me. "Is now a good time to talk about why you and Graham have to save your asses?"

A knock sounded at the door before it opened and Graham let himself in, eyeing the both of us before shooting dark daggers at Duncan.

"Do you always just let yourself into places you're not wanted?" Duncan quipped.

"This is my apartment, asshole."

"Guys, we aren't doing this today," I chided. "Graham, I wrote everything down in the notebook there. Can you look at it and make sure we're not missing anything?"

The further he made his way into the apartment, the more noticeable the bruise under his eye became. It did nothing to diminish his handsome features. He didn't nod or respond verbally, only lifted the notebook and reviewed it as he poured himself a cup of coffee too.

I turned my focus back to Duncan. "Detective Reid, we met him the night Dr. Keller was arrested. Do you remember?" He nodded. "Well, he met with us yesterday and said he and other people down at the station weren't buying our story of how we knew so many details about the crimes she committed. He said we had last night to prove our ability, or he was going to arrest us and bring us in for further investigation."

Duncan's bare shoulders tensed; his green eyes became dim. "He can't do that, can he? You're innocent."

"No shit, we're innocent" Graham snarked. I shot

him a 'play nice' look. "But that's why you've got to go." Graham looked to me. "Reid will be here within the hour."

"If you think I'm leaving here without her, you've lost your fucking mind."

I jumped up, almost spilling my coffee ready to throw it at both of them. "This is what we're going to do. Duncan, could you please call Olivia and let her know that I'm fine and that you're with me. I don't think I ever turned my phone back on after it died yesterday, but I know when I call her, she'll have a scolding I'm not ready to hear yet." I faced Graham, "I need you to check over those notes and make sure we're not missing anything. I'm not going to jail because some grumpy, closed minded, detective doesn't believe us. And for me, I'm going to shower. I expect the both of you to behave like grown men while I'm gone."

\*\*\*

With tempers only mostly extinguished, we waited for Detective Reid. Duncan and I wore the same clothes we had on yesterday, while Graham opted for his usual style, a crisp white button down and dress slacks. He had patients to attend to later this afternoon and we still needed to talk about Tawny before we went in.

A heavy thud-thud-thud interrupted the tense quite that filled the apartment. Graham stood, dusted imaginary dust of the tops of his slacks and opened the door. "Detective, it's…" His greeting was interrupted with a gruff voice.

"Graham Keller, you're under arrest for conspiracy to commit heinous crimes – "

*No!* "Wait!" I rushed to the door as Graham was being spun around, an officer in a black uniform locking his wrists in cuffs. "We had a deal!"

"That's right. We did. That deal was to prove to me that you two have the abilities you say you do. Well, guess what. I saw neither of you in my dreams last night. But I will see you in a cell."

A second officer entered the apartment and bound my wrists behind my back. I heard Graham threatening to call his lawyer from the corridor as he was being pulled near the elevator. Duncan had already started to charge my way, his green eyes holding an anger I feared would make this situation much worse.

"The notebook! Duncan, the notebook." Clarity filled his expression as he flipped through the pages.

"A hit and run?" he questioned.

I nodded franticly, as the officer started walking me backwards towards the door. "A hit and run. A thirteen-year-old daughter, and ice cream?" Duncan read my highlighted notes with confusion.

"What'd you say?" Reid and his deep grumpy forehead lines turned to face Duncan.

"We *were* there." My eyes narrowed in on him, demanding him to look at me. The officer who had tightened the cuffs around my wrists had the decency to stop dragging me when I spoke. "We saw you, sulking in a corner, not doing your damn job." I made no effort in hiding the disdain in my voice. Maybe I should have, considering the position I was in.

His gray eyes blinked under his creased brow. I

could tell I had his attention.

"While everyone else was busy, trying to find the driver who killed that poor woman, you were in the corner, having an existential crisis. You said it was your first scene."

And like a punch to the gut would drop a man to his knees, Ried's hardened and hell-bent expression fell. "Release them."

I wasn't sure I had heard him correctly, but everyone stilled at his words. When no one complied, he repeated himself. "I said," raising his voice, "release them."

Metal clicked against metal, and I heard the lock twist and release as the cold cuffs fell from my wrists. I rubbed the bite away and Graham entered back into the apartment, rubbing his wrists too.

"Your backup is no longer requested, gentlemen." The officers nodded and retreated to the elevator. Detective Reid pushed himself inside and shut the door behind him. He was quite for a long time. I backed further up, inching my way closer to Duncan before I felt the support of his hard chest behind me.

"So, do you believe us now?"

"Unfortunately," Reid grunted. "I don't understand how, but there's no way either of you would have known about that case. My name was never in any of the reports, and it happened back in Portland."

Graham slowly made his way beside Duncan and me where we stood in front of Reid. It seemed that none of us wanted to make any sudden movements for fear of winding up back in handcuffs.

"That case haunts me. I spent weeks helping my

fellow officers hunt down that driver. I was sick with grief because I felt like I failed the girl. I failed at bringing her mother's killer to justice. Until one day, we got a tip. The diver was found trying to dispose of his car at a scrap yard. When we brought him in for questioning, he was adamant that he didn't hit her, that instead, she fell in front of his car." Reid dragged his hand down his chin. "We of course thought he was a liar and booked him anyway. It wasn't until one of the officers re-examined the crime scene photos. The victim wasn't laying on the sidewalk. She was in the street. If the driver had hopped the sidewalk like the daughter had said, then the sidewalk is where her body should have been. When the girl was brought back in for questioning, her story didn't exactly line up to what she told us the first time." He cleared his throat and placed his hands on his hips beneath his round waist. "In short, she lied. The truth was that she pushed her own mother in front of that car."

My hand shot up and covered my mouth, shocked by the unexpected truth. No wonder he's such a hard ass. I probably would be too if I was duped by a thirteen-year-old girl.

"Are we good now?" I asked hopeful. "Cleared of all suspicion?"

Reid nodded, "I'll let my superiors know. As of now, you two have been cleared and are no longer considered suspects."

I felt Duncan's chest deflate and he rubbed his hands down my arms.

"I'll be in touch if we need your assistance on any matters related to the crimes committed by Dr. Jamie Keller."

"Thank you," Graham and I said in unison.

Detective Reid nodded his head to the room and turned to leave. But he did a double take when he looked to Graham. His eyes flicked to Duncan. "Hm." He looked to me next. "I assume that's because of you?" He said, pointing to the noticeable bruises and cuts decorating Graham and Duncan's face.

"I cannot be held responsible for other people's actions," I said sarcastically.

He just shook his head and looked at each of them. "You both look like shit." He turned back to Graham, "You might want to ice that shiner. Looks like he got you pretty good."

I heard Duncan snicker behind me. Graham's dark eyes, clouded with fury and annoyance, narrowed and shot to Duncan.

Detective Reid shook and scratched his head, "We'll be in touch." He turned a final time and left the apartment. The three of us released a breath as the air became lighter. I was thankful not to have a looming arrest hanging over my head anymore.

# Chapter 23

## Heidi

"Heidi, could I talk to you for a moment?" Graham called from the back of the living room near the bookshelf.

I placed my hands on Duncan's chest, "Give me a second, okay?"

"Actually, I'll give you two some space." He pressed his full lips to my knuckles as he brought my hand to his lips. The warmth and dampness of his lips, surrounded by the scruffiness of his facial hair sent a tingle across it. "I'll go grab us some lunch. I should run an errand anyway while I'm here. Kathrine's office isn't far from here."

"Okay. I'll see you when you get back?"

"You'll see me when I get back." He pressed his lips to mine before shooting Graham a warning look. He pulled on his boots and slipped out the door.

I walked over and slumped down on the couch, "What's up?"

He sat down on the opposite end, leaned forward and rested his elbows on his knees. "Could you come with me to meet Tawny later today? I planned to ask her about the dream last night."

"How do you know it was even Tawny?"

"I've Connected with her. On a few occasions, she's the younger, eleven-year-old version of herself. I'm curious to know how she's connected to that house. It's the same one we saw before, right?"

I nodded. "It is. But I haven't figured out its significance yet. I've had that dream before, but I can't remember how it ends. And now," thoughts ran rapid in my mind, "Tawny's there. Earlier in the night, I saw her in one of Duncan's dreams."

"Really?" Intrigued, Graham sat back on the couch, lifting his chin slightly, like he was mapping the details in mid-air.

\*\*\*

Graham sat on a wooden chair he retrieved from Tawny's dining room. Tawny and I each took up a cushion on her couch. "I'd like to ask you about any dreams you remember from last night." Graham readied his pen for her response.

Tawny was suffering from anxiety and night terrors. There were days when she was incapable of leaving her house. Today was one of those days. It's not in the norm for Graham to make house visits, but this was an exception.

Graham had been Connecting with her to help her through the trauma of her attack. Since she never saw her attacker, an arrest could never be made. Graham had also mentioned that her dreams were indicative of a lot more than the sneak attack she's shared with us, but Tawny hadn't opened up to him about anything else yet. He was hoping that bringing me along would help her be more forthcoming.

Something bigger than us was happening and we needed to figure it out. How could Tawny, Duncan, and I be connected? What were we missing here?

Tawny twisted her lips and started to chew on

them.

"Tawny," Graham spoke softly, "you don't have to share anything you don't want to… but the more you share, the better we'll be able to help you."

Tawny considered his words, "I didn't dream last night. Or I don't remember it if I did."

*If she didn't dream, was the dream about the house mine?*

"But you're right, there is more that I should share."

I could see her visibly shaking. I wasn't sure if it was improper etiquette or not, but I scooted closer to her and wrapped my arm around her as if I was trying to warm her up. "Really. You only need to share *if* you want to. *When* you want to."

She nodded and I felt the quakes of her shoulders soften. Pulling a calming breath between her lips, she spoke. "My mom –" a shudder ran through her again, her voice raspy from the sudden emotion in her throat. "My mom was murdered." She wiped her nose with the heel of her hand. "The same night of my attack," she sniffled.

Graham's pen made movement across the paper as Tawny recovered slightly from the admission. "Was her murderer caught?" Tawny shook her head, tears threating her bright blue eyes. "Did the police think these crimes were committed by one person, or two?"

"Cops didn't come up with shit for evidence for either crime," she nearly spat. "Said they didn't have any leads for either."

"Your mom's murder, were you able to process that though therapy also?" She nodded. "And you've been handling your anxiety successfully this whole time." He stated to himself as if he was in a thought. "I want you to think back to before these night terrors began. Before the first time you felt like someone was following you. What happened?"

Tawny sat silent and still for a long moment until her eyes grew wide. "I – I thought I ran into someone I knew. Someone from my past that I haven't seen in a very long time."

"So, this person was a stranger?"

"Yes. But there was something familiar about their eyes that I couldn't shake. The longer I thought about it, the more absurd it sounded. It would be impossible for it to have been who I thought it was."

"Did this person know you before or after the traumas you've endured?"

"Before."

"Could you tell us how?"

She shook her head absentmindedly, "It was just someone that I grew up with." Her head dropped slightly, and guilt coated her tone. "I hadn't thought about them in a long time."

Graham sat quietly as he finished his notes. "My theory is this: you thinking you saw someone from that time of your life may have been the very trigger that caused these night terrors. And if that's true, we now have an opportunity to change our approach for your treatment."

We spent the next fifty or so minutes reviewing and processing any dreams or terrors she had this week. The first few dreams she described were all related to the attack. But then she described a dream she had where she was a kid again, in her bedroom listening to her mom being smacked around.

This must have been the dream Graham was referring to earlier. Could she have come from a home where domestic violence was an issue? And if there was domestic violence, then maybe that person was also responsible for her mom's murder. *But if that was the case, why did she say the police didn't have any leads?*

And I still wasn't sure how she wound up in Duncan's hallway dream and how she wound up in my house dream. None of the dreams she described were either of those.

On the way out the door I had a nagging question in the back of my mind. I contemplated asking or not, but just as I approached the door, one foot out, I stopped and turned back towards her. "Tawny," my sudden change of direction slightly startled her, "do you by chance know anyone named Duncan?"

Her eyebrows pulled down, confused by the question. "No, I don't know anyone named Duncan."

"Alright. Thank you." I heard her lock the door behind me as I followed Graham down the pathway from her town home.

"Why'd you only offer his first name?" Graham asked, questioning why I didn't give Tawny Duncan's last name.

"Duncan's adopted. Johnson is his adoptive parents' name. So, it wouldn't have meant anything to her anyway." Reaching the car, we both got in and pulled off, heading back to the apartment. "So, what do you think? How could she be in not just my dream, but Duncan's also?"

Graham shrugged his broad shoulders and looked

briefly over at me before turning his attention back to the road. "Honestly, I have no idea. This is all uncharted territory. But I have a theory."

I stared at him expectantly. "Which is…?"

"What if you somehow Connected with her and pulled her into your other Connections."

"That's a thing?" I asked, overwhelmed at the thought of how that could be possible. Could we pull people from their own dreams and place them in another Connection entirely?

"I don't know. I'm just saying it was a thought. I plan to explore it a bit more, but if something like that were to be possible, I would think she would need to be dreaming also, or at least in a R.E.M state."

I slumped against the seat, closing my eyes, organizing and calming the thoughts, too exhausted to offer Graham acknowledgement of his statement.

"So," he cleared his throat. "How far along are you?"

My eyes slammed opened, and I turned to face him. "How did you know?" There was no need in hiding it or trying to skirt around it.

"Besides your wildly erratic mediating tactics, albeit enjoyable," a devilish smirk flicked on his lips, and I felt myself turn red, "you've been hugging yourself a lot. But not for your own comfort, for the protection of what's growing under your abdomen. I noticed it first at the apartment yesterday. Then during our Connection with Reid. Then again in there with Tawny when she mentioned that her mother had been murdered."

"Well, aren't we observant," I said only partly sarcastic. I hadn't even noticed my reaction to the news Tawny shared.

He laughed. "It's my job to be observant, Heidi." His eyes fell to my lips but quickly snapped back to the road ahead of him. "Heidi... I need to be honest with you."

I swallowed hard. Hardly anything good ever came after those words.

"I have feelings for you." His admission was rushed. "You consume all my free thoughts. I don't know if that will ever change. And believe me, if Duncan fucks this up, I will shamelessly try and swoop in. Even if for a rebound. I will take you in anyway or capacity you allow."

The unexpected words had me sweating from his raw honesty and my blushing. It was unlike Graham to waver from his even temperament.

"But" he punctuated his own ramblings. "I will not interfere with a man and his family."

I smiled appreciatively at him. I didn't think he understood how serious Duncan and I were when he first asked about our relationship. Hell, I didn't know we were *this serious* either, but my heart had and would always belong to Duncan. Maybe this would be the truce Graham and Duncan needed. Sucks that it was only because I was knocked up, but the two of them would have had to learn how to get along eventually. Neither of them would be leaving my life any time soon.

# Chapter 24

## Heidi

As I pulled into my driveway later that evening, I shifted my car in park, rested my forehead on the top of my steering wheel, and released an overdue sigh.

The past two days had been overwhelming to say the least. I had yet to bring my sister, or my parents for that matter up to speed on the recent developments of my life.

I need to figure out the Connection Tawny had to Duncan and I.

I needed fresh clothes.

And I needed to pee. I was only going to be here at my house long enough for me to shower, pack a bag, and head over to Duncan's.

Once he returned with lunch earlier, we had just enough time to enjoy the fairly decent fish tacos he brough back. Duncan said he got fish because it's good for the baby. He also brough back prenatal vitamins. I hadn't had a chance to pick any up after my appointment. Or between trying to prove my innocence, refereeing a battle between the machos, or getting cuffed for crimes I didn't commit.

But, at the end of the day, I was able to tell the man I loved that I was pregnant with his baby, and he didn't run. That didn't change the fact that we needed to bring our walls down. Together.

I hadn't forgotten what Olivia said – I still needed closure. I didn't think I would be able to fully forgive

Duncan for breaking my heart the way he did if I didn't.

From my purse sitting beside me in the passenger seat, my phone vibrated. Without moving my head from its resting place, I reached for my bag and blindly groped at it until I felt the cold glass screen. I brought it under my gaze. Olivia.

I pressed the green accept button then hit the speaker button, laying the phone on the seat between my thighs. "Hey." My tired voice barely held the syllable.

"Heidi! I just heard Duncan's truck drive past. Does that mean you're home too?" The panic in her tone sent guilt straight to my gut.

"Yeah. I just pulled up."

Her relief was audible as she blew out a breath on her end of the line. "Good. Want me to come over?"

"No, that's alright. I'll be heading over to Duncan's in a bit."

"Oh."

"Not that I don't want to see you," I clarified. "I just need to smooth things over with Duncan. A lot has happened that I need to address and move on from."

"Oh?" her tone went from low to high. "Is Heidi Miller saying she wants to have an adult conversation instead of allowing her thoughts to fester and overwhelm her?"

I smirked at her teasing tone. "The things I do for love."

"It will all work out. But the two of you need to definitely work on your communication skills. When he showed up here the other night, he had me worried that something happened to you. Turns out, he didn't know diddly squat about where you were or why you were in the city."

Annnnd here came the lecture.

"You're going to be a... mother," she whispered. "You can't keep doing things for the sake of 'Heidi'. You have a family to think about now."

"I know, Olivia." She didn't know that Duncan stormed off and that's why I went to the doctor alone, so I was trying to contain my irritation with her. "But that's part of what I need to smooth over with Duncan. And I love you, but it's getting late, and I'm exhausted. I need to head inside to get my things together since I'm staying over at Duncan's tonight."

Whatever words she had lined up to say next, she quickly dismissed them. "Alight," she said with a small huff. "I'm glad your home and safe. I love you."

"Love you, too."

\*\*\*

Entering Duncan's house, I noticed a small cardboard box sitting under the coffee table in the living room.

He was making his way up the hallway by the time I shut the door behind me. His broad shoulders and toned torso were all that I could focus on. Never mind the green eyes that were burning through me at the moment. I had to lick my lips to remoisten them, trying to remember why I came over here.

Oh yeah. *Why'd you break my heart at the tender age of seventeen, you handsome jerk.*

The gap disappeared between us. He tilted my chin up, capturing my lips with his own. "Feel better?"

Blinking up at him, I muttered, "Huh?"

He tucked a damp tendril behind my ear. "Earlier, before we left, you said you weren't feeling well. That your nausea had returned. Are you feeling better?"

"Oh, yeah." He took my bag, and I kicked my shoes off by the door. I followed him to his room and leaned against the door jamb. He sat my bag down on the foot of the bed. "It comes and goes mostly. I haven't thrown up too many times thankfully." I watched him take the toiletries out of my bag and move them to the bathroom. "The doctors said that's normal though and hopefully it'll ease up in a few weeks."

"That's good," he said as I watched him move about his room, emptying two drawers before assessing his closet.

"Did you lose something?"

"No," he shrugged casually. "Just making a sure you have a place to put some of your stuff."

I straightened up from the door jamb, "My what? What stuff?"

"Your stuff," he said simply. "Anything you want to keep here. *If* you want to keep it here." He squeezed casually past me with a knee-melting smile and made his way down the hall.

I spun on my heels and followed, hoping he'd elaborate a bit more as he entered the kitchen. When he didn't, I stopped and stared at him, willing him to explain.

Instead, he opened one of the cabinets and looked at me over his shoulder. "You hungry? I'm making oatmeal." I hadn't answered but he pulled down two bowls anyway. He then walked over to the small pantry and asked, "Brown sugar maple, or plain?"

"Duncan. What are you talking about 'my stuff'?"

He pulled out a pack of each and sat them on the counter then grabbed the milk from the fridge. "I mean, your stuff. You have stuff at your house, and now, if you want to have stuff at my house too, you can." With a tick, tick, tick and whoosh, a little blue flame roared to life under the pot of milk he just poured. "This isn't a decision you need to make right now. Or any time soon. I'm simply saying that you have a place here."

I approached him at the stove and leaned my hip up against the counter. "Duncan, I don't want to sound dismissive of your gesture, but I think we have bigger things to talk about."

If we were going to move into our future, we needed to put our past on the table. There had always been something he's held back from me, and I wanted to understand. I couldn't give him all my love if he couldn't give me all of his. "I don't think I can fully move on until I understand what happened. Why you left me the way you did back then. I don't want to be blindsided, especially with this baby on the way."

Duncan stirred the milk, calming the little bubbles that started to roll, and nodded. "I know."

"So, can we talk about it, or are you going to run again?" The low light being emitted from the hood above the stove did little to hide his wince. My words were harsh and uncalled for, but they bubbled up before I could stop them.

Duncan turned the knob on the stove and poured milk into each of the bowls before emptying an oatmeal pack into each and stirring. "I'm done running."

He placed a spoon in each bowl and carried them into the living room as I followed behind, resting them on the coffee table in front of the couch. He motioned for me to take a seat first. He pulled the box from under the table and sat it on top. Eyeing the box, he said, "I'm not sure where to even begin." He then sat back on the couch, his knees spread wide, and dropped his folded hands in his lap.

He sat silently for a moment before inhaling, then on his exhale, it all came pouring out.

# Chapter 25

## Duncan

"I don't have any memory of my life before I was adopted by the Johnsons. The orphanage didn't have any details either. My parents were registered as foster parents for the state but had never fostered before. They received a call that a young and possibly mute boy needed a family. They made the drive to Mallard Bay to meet me, and they said that was it. The moment they saw me, they knew I was going to be a perfect addition to the family. I came home with them that night."

I saw Heidi momentarily look away from me to the steaming bowls of oatmeal on the coffee table. Then I heard her stomach growl as she looked apologetically at me. I pointed to the bowl on the left. "That's the brown sugar maple," knowing that was the one she'd want. Her eyes squinted with an appreciative yet apologetic grin.

She reached and pulled the bowl to her, careful not to palm the scalding bottom. She gave it a quick stir and blew on a spoonful. "I'm sorry. Please continue." She wrapped her mouth around the spoon and an unexpected rush of desire landed on the tip of my cock.

Shaking away the thought, I continued. "My adoption wasn't finalized until about eight months later. But in that time, my parents decided to give therapy a shot. Everything they had tried to pull me out of my shell had failed. I was ultimately diagnosed with selective mutism."

Her brow arched, asking me to define what I meant. "Basically, meaning that I *could* talk. I had the physical ability to do so, I just didn't. The therapist said it was likely a response to trauma. For those first two years of my life with them, they ran me back and forth to those appointments trying to 'heal' me. Once I started talking and was holding conversations regularly, they felt it was important to transition my education from homeschool to public school."

I took a more comfortable seat, sitting sideways on the couch to face her, resting my elbow on the back of it. "I remember feeling so nervous and begging them not to send me. But they dropped me off anyway, filling me with words of encouragement. Their hopes were that with therapy, I'd also be able to remember what happened before I wound up at the orphanage. But my memory never came."

"Did the orphanage not have any details? I mean, did they just wake up with a baby on their doorstep?"

I chuckled at her guess. "No, but from what my parents have told me, I was at another orphanage before winding up in Mallard Bay."

"Did that orphanage have any details?"

"My parents called them, but they didn't have the records for me either. Apparently at the time, that particular orphanage was overcrowded and had to place several children in other homes. They said my file could have gotten misplaced."

"How does someone loose – you know what, not the point of this conversation. I'm sorry. I'll stop interrupting you now."

I placed my hand on her knee and gave it a reassuring squeeze. "I continued therapy for a few more months after starting school in case I experienced any sort of regression. With the exception of not being able to remember any time before the Johnsons, everyone was in agreement that I was on the mend and as long I was socializing well with my peers, I was safe to discontinue further treatment. As I got older, I had asked my parents a few times over the years if they were able to find any new details about my birth parents. The answer was always no. But on my fifteenth birthday, they gave me a box."

Heidi's eyes flicked from me to the box on the coffee table."

"The contents were meaningless. Still are. I would look at them from time to time, trying to evoke some sort of memory but that never happened. Nothing in my life, nothing in therapy, nothing in the box, ever induced the slightest reminder. Not until you told me that you loved me."

Her eyes wide, mouth agape. "I don't understand. How could I have triggered something from your past?"

I just shrugged. "I don't know. But as soon as you said it, you unlocked something in my mind. 'You're not worthy of love' was all that I heard. And it's all that I've been able to hear ever since."

Those beautiful hazel eyes of hers were glassy as she searched my face for understanding. Unfortunately, I didn't have any to offer.

"I was always quite about my past, because I didn't know it – not because I didn't want to share it with you. I feel incredibly lucky to have had this community accept me as one of their own, but I always felt guilty. I always felt somewhat like a stranger. I worried that if I brought it up, people would forget that I wasn't a true part of this town. And I didn't want to lose another family."

Tears streamed down her face now. I removed the empty bowl from her hand and sat it down next to my still full bowl before drying her cheeks with my thumbs.

"I always felt like you wouldn't let me in because you didn't trust me. And if you didn't trust me, then maybe you didn't really love me the way I loved you."

I shook my head, "I couldn't let you in because I couldn't get in myself." I took her hands in mine, "I was going to tell you that I loved you that day. The whole hike up to our spot, I had to fight the words from blurting out. I was so nervous; I wasn't sure if you felt the same way. But then we got there, and you pulled out that little foil packet from your bra. I thought I was hallucinating," I said with a chuckle. "How could I have been so lucky to have the girl of my dreams want to share her first time with me? Then you said it. The three words that I had been holding on the tip of my tongue from the day I met you, flowed so effortlessly from your lips."

I brought her knuckles to my mouth, pressing my lips hard against them. My eyes squeezed shut from the memory of that day shooting to the forefront of my mind. How the road to my future crumbled so easily, leaving me only a haunted path to my past.

"That voice in my head sounded more like a

threat. Like, if I were to keep pulling at it, it'd destroy me. Destroy you. And that's why I ran. I didn't know what hid in the darkness of my memory, but from that day forward I could feel it. It was evil. And that wasn't something I was willing to share with you. Whatever the burden, it was mine alone."

Heidi climbed over onto my lap. Her forehead pressed to mine; she wrapped her hands around the back of my neck. "Duncan, you are more than worthy of love." She planted a soft kiss on my lips. "Whatever is hidden up there, it doesn't define you." Another kiss. "I'm sorry I just let you walk away." This time, her kiss was relentless. It was hard and sad.

I couldn't tame the bulge building under my sweatpants, seeking the warmth it craved. "Heidi," I pulled away from her gently. "I'm sorry for ever making you feel like I didn't love you. It couldn't be further from the truth. You brought me back to life."

Heidi's lips devoured mine again. Her tongue parted my lips as she pulled me in deeper. She pulled away only long enough to pull her shirt over her head. She reached behind her back and unhooked her bra. She looked longingly at me, her hazel eyes warming me from the inside out.

I brought my hands to her shoulders where her bra straps rested. Using the tips of my fingers, I slowly slid them down her arms, freeing her breasts. My cock was at full attention now, there was no use in fighting it. I dipped my head down and pulled a nipple between my lips and sucked before flicking my tongue across it.

She braced herself on my shoulders as her head fell back and she arched towards me. I moved to her other nipple, continuing my relentless flicking as she moaned, her sex grinding against my lap.

Never letting my mouth leave her breasts, I carefully lifted and flipped her over to lay her on the couch. Tucking my fingers into the waistband of her pants and panties, I pulled them both off her long legs and tossed them on the floor. Seeing her wet and ready for me pulled out a throaty groan. I rose and pushed down my sweatpants, my dick finally free to satisfy its appetite.

She threw her right leg over the back of the couch as she spread her other leg further apart, digging her heel into the cushion beneath her.

I rested my knee on the couch between her thighs and swiped two fingers between her slick folds. Her eyes shut and the sound of her husky moan pricked the head of my cock. Bringing the two fingers to my mouth, tasting her desire. My balls tightened.

Her chest heaved with anticipation, her thighs fell wider apart, her eyes landed desperately on my mouth. I knew exactly what she wanted.

Heidi watched as I lowered my head, lining up my mouth with her slit. She smelled incredible. Widening my tongue, I licked the entire length of her slit. Her hips bucked up, and her hands held my head in place.

"Right there," she whimpered. My tongue swirled around her clit, and I reached for her breasts. Rolling her nipples between my fingers, she let out a breathy sob and her release spilled onto my tongue.

The satisfied look in Heidi's eyes filled me with an odd sense of pride. I put that look on her face.

Rising back up, I held the shaft of my cock, lining my tip with her slick and swollen opening, stroking myself just once before I dove deep into her, causing her to let out a sultry cry. The sound washed over me in waves of ecstasy with each thrust. When I felt a deep and greedy need infect my pace, I tried to ease out of her and slow down. Instead, she shook her head with a devious smirk and wrapped her left leg around me, using it to slam me back inside of her.

Heidi reached her hands behind her head and held onto the arm of the couch, bracing herself from the punishing pace I set. Dipping my head, I captured one breast with my mouth and kneaded the other with my hand. Quick pants escaped her lips. When she tilted her hips down, I knew she was close. I reached my hand between us and circled my middle finger around her sensitive nub, rewarding me with another moan.

Her muscles tightened around me harder, and I timed my release with hers. I chased the first contraction of her orgasm with my own, causing her eyes to roll shut as she yelled my name through her gasps. "Duncan!"

With both of us spent, I slowed my pace to a gentle rock. Her eyes opened slowly, and she grabbed the side of my face. "I love you."

I dropped my head and kissed her smile, "I love you, too."

# Chapter 26

## Heidi

After cleaning myself up from the slippery mess between my thighs, I returned to my spot on the couch and wrapped myself in the blue crochet throw blanket that always laid on the arm of Duncan's couch. It didn't do much for warmth, but it was soft and provided me decent coverage to keep me comfortable enough.

Duncan returned with a fresh bowl of oatmeal. This time, he brought us each a glass of water too. He reached his large hand that was balancing both cups in his palm towards me. I carefully took one and took a sip. Duncan stood over me, smirking at me.

"What," I wiped my dry chin. "Did I spill it?"

"No. It's just that I can see your nipples." He wiggled his eyebrows at me, and I swatted his arm playfully.

"Would you like for me to cover up better?"

"Oh, don't do that. As a matter of fact, you could just remove the blanket completely."

I couldn't keep the smile from spreading across my face. "Well, if I did that, you would be too distracted to answer my question."

Duncan blew on his bite of oatmeal. "What question?"

I nodded toward the box under the coffee table. "Can I see what's inside?" He turned his head, gazing pensively at the box.

He nodded as he took a bite of his oatmeal. "There's not much in there." He reached forward to grab it then handed it to me as I sat slouched against the couch.

It hurt my heart knowing that his life before the Johnsons fit in this tiny box. Judging by the lightness of it, he was right, there wasn't much in here. Which only made my heart ache more. I pulled back the flaps and surveyed the items inside. A rock, a toy, a toothbrush, and a scrap of newspaper. "None of this holds any importance to you?" I asked as I pulled out the figurine and eyed it, unable to recognize the character.

He spoke around a bite of oatmeal, "Nope."

I replaced the figurine and pulled out the newspaper. My eyes scanned the words that stretched across it. Whoever cut the snippet wasn't very considerate. Most of the article was missing. The only prominent detail that could be made out was about a tornado tearing through a neighbourhood. I made a mental note to research more details about it another time. I flipped it over, curious if more of the article was on the back.

Eyes wide, I shot up from my slouched position at the image on the opposite side of the clipping. I studied the picture closer. Instead of the continuation of the article that I had expected, my eyes were locked on a black and white image of the same house that had appeared in my dreams.

"What is it?" Duncan asked when I sat up.

I flipped the clipping towards him, "This house. Do you know anything about it? Or why it's in your box?"

"No. I don't recall ever seeing that house before. Except in that picture. Why?"

"I've seen this house before." I shot to my feet and started to pace, pinching the crochet blanket under my arms to keep it in place, focusing on the image in my hand.

"How?" Duncan set his bowl down on the table in front of him and turned his attention to me.

"I mean, I've seen it in my dreams before. First on the night of the engagement then again last night." I paced a few more steps, replaying the conversation with Tawny earlier. I can't rule out that the dreams weren't hers, but she didn't remember them if they were. "Last night, did you have the hallway dream again?" He nodded his head. "Did you see anyone with you?"

"I don't think so."

I felt my face scrunch with curiosity, trying to connect all the pieces.

"What's going on in the beautiful mind of yours?"

I looked down at him, pausing my pace. I couldn't tell him about Tawny or that I saw her since it would interfere with patient confidentiality. He didn't know any more details about his past that could help me connect the dots either. So, the only conclusion I came to was, "I need to talk to Graham." Duncan tried to conceal the hurt and irritation in his eyes, but I caught it. "I'm sorry, Duncan. But there are things I'm not allowed to discuss with you."

He scoffed, "Wow." He grabbed the back of his neck with his hand and shook his head absently. "But you can discuss things with him?"

I didn't have a response. He was right to be

frustrated but I wouldn't be able to figure this out without Graham.

"I don't want him anywhere near this. It doesn't concern him."

"But he could help us. We could figure all this out. We can Connect and –"

"I don't want him anywhere near my dreams," he seethed. The disappointment on my face must have been obvious. "Heidi, I mean it. You and only you are allowed in here." He tapped a pointer finger to his temple.

"You know, he's the best chance we've got at figuring all this out. I don't know if I'll be able to do this on my own."

"No." His admonishment was curt and vexed. I noticed his chest was slightly puffed out too.

"Duncan, this macho shit between the two of you has to stop. I plan on having both of you in my life for a long time."

He dragged his hands down his face, unsuccessfully wiping away his aggravation before he rose to his feet. "He wants *you*. You know that right?"

I rolled my eyes. My hip popped out and I rested my hand on it, still keeping the blanked pressed to me. "It doesn't matter what he wants."

"He's the kind of guy who always gets what he wants. I don't know if I'll ever be completely okay with the two of you working together. The two of you, working so intimately together. That's a bond that the two of you will share forever. And I will forever be on the outside of that."

"Duncan, –"

"No, please let me get this out." He took a

moment to calm himself, dragging his hands through his hair. "In the past, having to see you with someone else, it stung, but deep down, in the pit of my gut, I knew that someday, you and I would find our way back to each other. The fear of losing you was never terminal. And I know how shitty that sounds. How selfish it sounds but at the end of the day, I was yours and nothing would change that. But with Graham in the picture, I'm not so sure anymore."

I took a seat back on the couch and patted the seat next to me for him to join me. I used the opportunity to securely wrap the blanket around me again.

There was an attraction to Graham in the beginning and there's no denying his handsome features, but my heart belonged to only one man. And he was the big oaf sitting next to me. "Duncan, Graham can't have what doesn't want him." That brought a twitch of a smile to his lips. "Graham and I are colleagues and friends. And you're right, our job can be intimate but our job, our ability, is bigger than us. I can't ask you to absolve your worries, I know that will take time. But what I will ask is that you try. It's what I'm asking of both of you."

I watched as some of the tension left his shoulders. He sat silent for a breath before the tension returned. "Then I need to know," he swallowed hard and tried to keep his eyes trained on mine. "Has anything happened between you too?"

I tried to keep my expression neutral to prevent him from making any assumptions. "Uh." How do I say, 'not technically, but we tried' without it sounding awful? I settled on, "Almost." My admission sounded more like a question as I winced from seeing the hurt in his eyes. "But it was before us and I was at the institute and there was this *one* dream – never mind, we don't need to get into that – and you had called to brake our 'friendship' – relationship – thing off and then Graham was there but you were in the back of my mind and before anything could happen *happen* I got super sick and had to throw up in the sink." I watched as his expression went from hurt to understanding to amusement as I blurted it all out. Catching my breath, I asked, "What's so funny?"

With a warm smile, Duncan scooted closer to me and placed his hands on either side of my stomach, threading his thumb through the holes of the blanket to make contact with my skin. He rubbed the edges of my belly with his thumbs and said proudly, "Look at my son, already protecting his mama."

His words made me wonder back to what the doctor said about how long I had been pregnant. Back at the institute, when I got sick the night I almost slept with Graham, I thought it was food poising from that awful bakery. But it was more likely a symptom of my pregnancy. I smiled at the sentiment that our baby was intervening on behalf of our relationship.

*Wait, did he say*, "Son? What makes you think it's a boy?" Immediately a memory was triggered as my mind played back the dream I had where Duncan and I were together, building a home, and he asked me a question about the nursery. He couldn't remember which shade of blue I picked for the walls.

Duncan shrugged, "Just a feeling." He sat staring at me for a moment, still rubbing his thumbs tenderly across my belly. "If you really think Grham can help, then I trust your judgement."

Relief washed over me. His journey to healing and discovering his past would be met with hurdles but the fact that he was letting me in, allowing me to help meant more than he would ever know. I leaned forward to plant a kiss on his lips then pressed my forehead to his and whispered, "Thank you."

# Chapter 27

## Heidi

I spent my morning catching Olivia up on everything that had happened the past few days. Being able to process the whirlwind of thoughts and emotions I've experienced the last seventy-two hours with her was cathartic.

Last night, after much deliberation between Duncan and I on when we should tell our parents about the baby, we decided to rip off the band aid and tell them today. We planned to drop by his parents' house unexpectedly during lunch since we knew my parents would be over there too.

Then, we were heading back to the city to meet with Graham, where he would assess Duncan's childhood trauma. We're hoping Graham will be able to uncover a few more details that would hopefully help us learn more about the house dream.

"Wish me luck," I said, as I stood from behind the counter. A wave of nausea hit me. I braced myself against the countertop and blew out a breath to calm it.

Olivia rubbed her hand over my back, "You've got this."

"Yeah, yeah," I teased as the nausea subsided. "I should be back in town tonight, but I don't know by what time. I'll check in with you later." I gave her a quick hug and grabbed my purse and headed out the door.

I pulled into Duncan's driveway and parked my car beside his truck. He was swinging in the porch swing when I got out of my car and peered up at him. "Ready to go tell our parents that you knocked me up?" I asked with a smirk.

Duncan gave me a handsome and sly grin as he descended the stairs. I shut the door and met him at the hood of my car where he bent down and gave me a kiss. "Absolutely."

When we got to the Johnsons' house, Duncan entered without knocking and I followed behind.

Mrs. Johnson appeared in the doorway of the dining room as we entered. "Oh hi! I thought I heard your truck pull up." She greeted me then Duncan with a hug at the door.

"Hey, Mom." Duncan kissed his mom's cheek.

She turned on her heels and motioned with her hand to follow, "Come on back. We just got lunch on the table and have plenty to go around."

I was suddenly nervous. What were my parents going to think? What were Duncan's parents going to think? I couldn't help but feel like this would be just one more disappointment my mom would add to the list of my previous infractions. I fell in line with Duncan's wide strides as if his body would shield me from their opinions.

"Look who decided to join us today," Mrs. Johnson said as we finally approached the dining room. A chorus of greetings from my parents and Mr. Johnson reached my ears as I sheepishly stepped from behind Duncan.

"Here, grab a seat," my dad said as he moved to the chair next to my mom on the opposite side of the table, allowing Duncan and I to sit next to each other on the side where he was originally sitting. Mr. Johnosn sat at one end of the table, and I assumed Mrs. Johnson would sit at the other.

Mrs. Johson returned with two plates and two glasses and sat them in front of us before taking her seat at the end of the table, opposite of Mr. Johnson.

My mom filled our glasses with water from the pitcher on the table. I watched the slices of cucumber and lemon float around, flirting with the rim of the pitcher as the water flowed from it into our glasses.

"Thank you," I said to the room. I couldn't quite bring myself to make eye contact with anyone. My heart raced with worry of how they were going to take the news. I was also trying to come to terms with the inevitable whispers that would start because of this. Gossip spread faster than germs around here.

"So," Mom started, as she began placing a few of the pinwheel sandwiches on her plate. "What brings you kids by today?"

Duncan and I looked at each other. I searched his face for any hesitation but found none. He placed his hand on my knee and gave it a gentle squeeze before leaving it there, grounding me with support and assurance.

I cleared my throat, "Well –" I croaked. I took a soothing gulp from my water, hydrating my dry throat and mouth. I noticed then that everyone was staring expectantly at me. I placed my hand on top of Duncans, tucking my fingers under his palm. I took one more glace at each of their unsuspecting faces before closing my eyes and blurting, "I'm pregnant."

I said it so fast, I worried no one understood me.

My eyes were squeezed shut, fearful of seeing my mom's expression. When no one said anything, I peeked through one eye at everyone.

What were they thinking? They each sat quietly looking from me to Duncan, then their glances darted between each other. I squeezed Duncan's hand, ready to just walk out of there to pretend like none of this even happened.

That's when I noticed my mom's mouth quiver before her hand rushed to cover it.

*Fuck. Here it comes.*

I watched Mrs. Johnson bring a napkin to the corner of her eyes, dabbing gently.

I couldn't make out either expression from Dad or Mr. Johnson.

"Oh, Heidi, honey," my mom finally said through a shaky voice. "Congratulations!"

*What?*

"We're going to be grandparents!" Mrs. Johnson squealed.

"Wait," I peered at everyone under a suspicious eyebrow. "You're not mad?"

"How could we be mad with a baby on the way?"

"Well, we aren't married for starters."

Mrs. Johnson flicked her wrist, "Will being married change how the two of you plan to love and care for the baby?"

I searched her face, confused by her question. "No."

"Okay then, it's the love that makes a family, not your relationship status."

"Exactly," my mom surprisingly agreed. "Will people around town talk about it? Absolutely. But will that change things? Not at all."

I turned to my dad and Mr. Johnson who sat silently. "Dad, what are your thoughts?"

Emotion welled in his eyes as he took a shaky breath and smiled. "My baby is going to have a baby." He used his napkin to wipe his nose.

Duncan turned to Mr. Johnson, "Dad, what about you?"

"I think the two of you just gave me one more reason to kick cancer's ass."

Light-hearted laughter erupted from each of us, and the moms stood, stretching their arms towards us for hugs. It wasn't until I felt my mom's arms wrap around my shoulders that I allowed myself to cry. I hadn't realized how much stress I had been carrying around, terrified to tell her. And now that it was here and she was *hugging* me, I felt so overwhelmed at the unexpected response.

She has always wanted this for us – to be married with kids and home. I guessed two out of three wasn't bad.

# Chapter 28

## Duncan

My parents were happy. Genuinely happy to become grandparents. Even though this baby wasn't technically their blood, they already loved it. Just like they loved me.

A realization washed over me that, no matter what we're able to uncover about my past, nothing would change the fact that the Johnsons were my *real* parents. And whatever happened before wouldn't change how they felt about me. I would always be their son.

Heidi was right – whatever was hiding in my mind's shadows didn't define me or my relationships.

The taillights clogging the highway finally thinned out as we neared the exit for the institute. We stuck around for about an hour after we ate lunch with our parents, and we wound up getting caught in rush hour traffic. It was lost on me as to why anyone would enjoy living here. I'd be miserable having to battle this shit Monday through Friday. Thankfully, the institute was just two exits down.

I was still coming around to the idea of asking for Graham's help. He irked my nerves, but Heidi asked for me to try to get along, and that's what I was going to do. *Try.*

However, I'd be lying if I didn't get a sliver of satisfaction from knowing that Heidi and I would always be in his face. Any time she'd need to be around Graham, he would be reminded of the relationship, the love, and the child that we shared. And that it was me that she shared those things with. Not him.

Finally, we pulled into the parking lot of the Keller Institute and parked. Heidi, having spent most of the trip down here busy looking stuff up on her phone, finally put it away and beamed at me before leaning across the middle of the seat and planting a big kiss on my lips. With delighted surprise, I asked, "What was that for?"

Her smile stretched ear to ear, she half shrugged her shoulders. "Nothing. I'm just glad you're letting me help you with this."

"Thank you for wanting to help me."

My phone rang, interrupting the moment. Ronny's name flashed on the screen. "Meet you inside? Ronny's calling."

"Okay." She pecked my cheek before hopping down out of the truck and skipping away.

"Hey, man."

"Hey, bro! Sorry I missed your call earlier, but I spoke to Mom – congratulations!"

I could hear Ronny's smile through the phone. "Thanks, I'm still in awe. I'm going to be a father."

"And a damn good one too."

*I hope so.* "I appreciate that. Mom was probably the most excited."

"I believe it," he said with a chuckle. "If there were enough babies in Mount Hopewell, she'd turn the house into a daycare. She's always been a sucker for their squishy cheeks and gummy smiles. How did Maxine take the news?"

"Surprisingly she was thrilled."

"Really? Wow. Can't say that I saw that coming."

"Yeah. None of us did. But when we left, she and Mom were thinking about what they wanted to be called."

"Well good. I'm glad it all went well."

"Me too. But hey, I'm in the city with Heidi and she's waiting for me. I'll talk to you tomorrow."

"Alright, bro. Congrats again. Tell Heidi for me too please."

"Will do. Talk to you later."

"Later."

I slid my phone into my front pocket as I stepped out of the truck. I saw Heidi standing on the sidewalk near the entrance of the institute talking with a blonde woman. I approached the spot where the two of them stood and lingered back a little as to not intrude on their conversation.

The blonde did a double take once she noticed my presence. Heidi turned, following the woman's eyes to me. "Oh." Her expression flicked with something unrecognizable. Like a thought rolled through her mind but if it did, she didn't let it linger. She motioned for me to stand next to her before wrapping her arm around me. "This is…" Heidi paused briefly, looking up at me, searching for something. "This is my boyfriend."

*Why did she hesitate?* I looked to the woman, ready to say hello, when I noticed her expression had fallen from friendly to hurt. I didn't even get a chance to introduce myself before she hurried off, disappearing around the corner into the parking lot. "Is she okay?"

Heidi had a curious look on her face as she looked forward and we began walking towards the entrance, "I hope so."

Once inside the institute, the receptionist at the desk nodded to Heidi. "Thanks," Heidi nodded back. She led me down the hallway to an office with a mostly closed door. She quickly tapped her knuckles against the door before opening it and ushering me inside. "Hey. So, we just saw Miss Fletcher on our way in." She shut the door behind her before taking a seat in front of the desk. I took the seat next to her.

"So, you did," Graham said as she sat back in his chair, crossing his ankle over his knee. "How'd it go?" The look on his face made it feel like he was asking a different question.

Heidi's bemused expression cleared as she responded. "She couldn't get to her car fast enough."

Graham nodded. "We'll. Let's go ahead and get started." He clicked his pen and pulled a white pad of paper into his lap, resting it against the top of his thigh. "I'm going to start with asking you a series of questions to help –"

I held my hand up, interrupting him. "This isn't my first rodeo. I know how this works." I felt Heidi's glare burn the side of my face. *Shit*. This was going to be harder than I thought. The way he seemed to be communicating with her telepathically irked me.

"Okay, that's fine. We'll just get right into it then. What's the earliest memory you can recall?"

I sighed, slightly annoyed that I would have to bare my soul to this asshat. "Uh, I remember meeting the Johnsons."

"Where?"

"The orphanage." *Obviously*. Where else would I have met them?

"What'd the orphanage look like?"

"Huh?"

"The orphanage where you met the Johnsons. Can you describe it?"

I recalled the memory in my mind. I see the Johnsons; they're sitting in the floor with me. But that's all I saw. I tried to think about any day prior, but it was all black, a dark abyss with a trove of secrets. "I uh, I can't."

Graham scribbled something on the paper. "What's a memory you remember after that?"

"Meeting my brother, Ronny at our home in Mount Hopewell."

"And your memories from that point forward are intact, correct?"

"Yes."

"Good." He scribbled something across his pad. "Now what I'd like you to do is think back to any time where an unknown memory tried to present itself, even if it only felt like an itch in your mind and you couldn't fully grasp it."

I thought about the first time Heidi told me she loved me. How it loosened a dark reminder. I looked over at Heidi, sorrow stretched across her face, knowing she had the same memory in her mind. "The first time Heidi told me she loved me."

It was subtle but I saw Graham still himself for just a second. I smirked internally. "Why do you think that would have triggered a memory? What transpired before she… said that?"

A shit eating grin started on my lips. If he wanted

to hear it, I'd happily tell him.

"Oh, I don't think we have to share that detail," Heidi said eyeing my expression.

"It could be important to the situation. No detail is too small," Graham rebutted.

Heidi's head dropped to her hand to shield her from the awkwardness. She didn't want to share such an intimate detail with him.

But I didn't mind. "We made love for the first time."

Again, like the words were too heavy to hold, his shoulders braced against them. "I see." A tint of red hid under his olive skin. He cleared his throat. "So, the memory, what was it of?"

"It wasn't of anything. Just a voice in the back of my head."

"What it'd say?"

It was my turn to hesitate. "It said that I wasn't worthy of love."

Graham made a note, "Was that all? Did that in turn trigger any other memory, or voice?"

I shook my head. "I'm not positive if it's even related to my forgotten memories. But my gut tells me it is."

I spent the next thirty minutes saying "I don't know" or "I can't remember" to the rest of his questions. Just as I had done when I was asked similar questions when I was a child. I couldn't remember anything, and whatever I had forgotten wanted to stay lost.

Graham placed the pad of paper and pen on his desk, interlaced his fingers and rested his elbows on it. "Well, Heidi might be right. We will likely be able to find more details during a Connection."

I supressed an aggravated grunt and eye roll. I had a feeling it would come to this too, but that didn't mean I was looking forward to this fucking guy running around in my mind.

But Heidi felt this would be beneficial and I trusted her intuition.

Into the darkness we go.

# Chapter 29

## Duncan

"Did that woman look familiar to you?" Heidi asked as we pulled out of the institute's parking lot.

"Which woman?"

"The one I was speaking to when we first got here."

"Oh. No." I looked over at her. "Why?"

"Just wondering. She seemed to be upset."

"Is she a patient there?"

She frowned, "I technically can't answer that."

I nodded and changed the subject. "Was everything okay back there?"

Graham asked that Heidi stay behind for a moment so they could 'chat'. I rolled my eyes at his tone when he told me to take a seat in the waiting room. I didn't miss the 'behave' look she shot Graham. It put a giddy smirk on my lips as I headed to the waiting room. I wasn't sure what they were talking about, but she was back there for about twenty minutes. I had started feeling antsy when she finally appeared from the hallway. It felt like he was holding her up intentionally just to piss me off.

"Mhm. Yep."

I didn't push further. If she had something she could share, I knew she would have.

When we finally got back into town, she asked if we could stop by her house first. When she reappeared on her front porch, she had a duffle bag slung over her shoulder.

"Taking a trip?" I teased when she hopped back up in the truck.

She laughed, "No. I just thought those empty drawers could use some filling."

My heart fluttered behind my chest, and I beamed at her. "Really?"

"Really." I pulled her palm to my lips and kiss the pad of her thumb. "I might need more drawers though," she said with a smile.

"You can have the whole dresser." The sound of her laugh wrapped around me as I backed out of her drive and headed home.

Arriving home, Heidi busied herself with filling her drawers. She wound up only needed one more, and I happily emptied it out for her. She also commandeered space on my bathroom sink. A toothbrush, a few hair elastics, and a tube of mascara laid freely on the righthand side. Then we ate supper and showered before settling into bed.

"If we don't get a good Connection tonight, don't worry. It could take a few tries before you're able to experience a true lucid dream. Did you want to refresh on any of the skills that we talked about earlier?"

On our way back from the city, and again over supper, Heidi went over a list of practices that they used at the institute to help patients achieve lucid dreams. None of them seemed overly complicated, but she warned that sometimes it took a little practice before someone experienced a successful lucid dream. "I don't think so. I'm going to follow your lead in there. I trust you."

A weak smile hit her lips. I could tell her thoughts were crowding her mind and I so desperately wanted to be able to help her the way she was helping me. Gently grabbing her chin to hold her gaze, attempting to calm her thoughts I asked, "Is there anything I can help *you* with?" Her eyebrow quirked up curiously. "I can tell you mind is running in overtime. Is there anything you could unload on me?"

She shook her head as a yawn stretched her smile. She slid into the covers before resting her head on the pillow. "I love you," she said with a sleepy smile.

"I love you too."

\*\*\*

*The yelling in the distance echoed around me. I took a few steps forward, but I remained in the same spot. The sound of glass shattering against something hard jolted me from the fog that had settled in my mind. There was something I was supposed to be doing.*

*But what?*

*"Stop it!"*

*My head swivelled in the direction of the plea.*

*"Please, stop!"*

*Again, my head twisted to find the source, but all I was met with was the plain walls of this dimmed hallway.*

*"Duncan!" I was embraced by an unexpected force. I noticed arms were slung around my arms and chest, squeezing me tight. "Please, Duncan. Feel me."*

*I looked down at the head that rested against my*

*chest. "Heidi?"*

*Her head shot up, locking those beautiful hazel eyes with mine. "Oh my gosh. Thank you thank you thank you thank you." Her hands found the sides of my face, forcing me to focus my gaze on hers. "Do you remember why we're here?"*

*Just then, I noticed a man standing not too far behind her.*

Graham.

*Then it all came back to me. Heidi and Graham were Connecting with me. "Yes." My head shook with clarity. "Yes, I remember now." Her forehead fell to my chest then her hands slid down and rested near my pecks. I wrapped my arms around her and rubbed her back.*

*"We've been trying to get your attention for a while. You really couldn't see us or hear us?" Graham asked.*

*All I could do was shake my head. This was an odd experience.*

*Graham wore an intrigued expression but quickly dismissed it. "Well, we should get started."*

*Heidi pulled herself away from me and I instantly became cold from where her body had just been. She tucked her hair behind her ear and smoothed her shirt. "Yes. We don't know how much time we'll have."*

*The sounds of destruction and terror continued to rip around us. "You can hear that, right?" I asked, holding my pointer finger upward, at nothing in particular, indicating to the sound around us.*

*"Yes," Heidi replied. "Someone needs help. Do you have any idea of who it could be?"*

"We need you to really think Duncan. Search the darkest corners of your mind and remember anything at all. Really try and feel this moment. Push though the discomfort."

I stood still, for what felt like a considerable length of time, trying to focus in on the unpleasant chaos. Trying to catalogue every sound, every crash, every plea. But still, my mind remained blank, just as it always had been. "There's nothing."

Heidi and Graham shared a look. Heidi was silently pleading. Graham's eyes were hard, but eventually, he conceded to whatever battle they were fighting.

"Okay. Plan B it is." Heidi said victoriously. She held out her hand to Graham then to me. "Hold on tight. We've never tried this before."

I squeezed her left hand, not ignorant to the fact that Graham was holding the other. She and Graham closed their eyes, so I did too.

When I felt Heidi's hand squeeze mine not even a minute later, I opened my eyes. And when I did, there was nothing to prevent me from stumbling backwards and falling flat on my ass.

The house, from the newspaper clipping was before me. The very house that had only lived in dusty black ink was brought to life.

"What is this?" I asked, fear, uncertainty, and confusion all circling in my gut.

Heidi extended her hand to pull me up. "This is my dream." Confusion, again, fell over my expression. "I think it's my dream anyway. I was certain until I saw the picture from your box. Now, I'm not so sure."

"How'd we get here?"

"That's something I'm still trying to figure out." Graham said. "We learn something new with each Connection. This is all completely uncharted as there's no existing science to fall back on." He looked longingly at Heidi. "This is all possible because of her. I have no doubt about it."

His affection towards her irritated me but I let it roll of me. They were trying to help me, and I needed to focus so their efforts weren't wasted. "So, now what?"

"We're going to go inside." There was something in Heidi's eyes that made me want to pull her to my chest. To protect her. It wasn't quite fear, but there was a glimmer of heavy uncertainty at the least.

I reached my hand towards her to offer her comfort, but if I was being honest, I needed it just as bad as she did. She accepted my hand and smiled. As if her touch fortified my will, I took the lead and lead her into the house. I heard Graham's footfalls bring up the rear.

I placed one boot on the first step, then the second, the third, then finally, the forth. My heart raced, unsure of what to expect as I crossed that threshold. But with Heidi by my side, I would be able to endure anything.

My only hope was that whatever waited for us beyond the door wouldn't push her away. Wouldn't devour me, forcing me back into a speechless, scared little boy.

I felt her straighten her shoulders. She looked to Graham then to me, nodding that it was now or never. With her hand still in mine, my wide strides *pulled us across the threshold. The three of us entered but only saw black, like we were standing freely in the night sky.*

*"What happens now?" I asked.*

*Graham and Heidi responded in unison, "I don't know."*

*We hesitated to take a step forward as fear crept in. I felt Heidi settle closer to me, wrapping her arm around mine. I felt her perch up on her tippy toes and whisper, "Whatever happens, I love you."*

*As if her words were the key to unlocking the darkness, our world around us spun and blurred, forcing me to close my eyes tight and secure Heidi to my side. I felt her hair whip against my arms and neck as the dark twisted into something wild.*

*"Stop it!" I heard again. "You're hurting her!" The crack of skin-on-skin contact forced my eyes opened. A tall man, dressed in black jeans and a leather jacket stood over a small blonde woman. His fist driving into her face, over and over again. Blood flung freely from his fist each time he reared his arm back. The woman's face was barely recognizable.*

*My chest expelled any air left in it when my eyes landed on the two kids in the corner of the kitchen. Children.*

*Two children sat, witnessing the assault that was unfolding before them. It was about that time when Heidi's body seized against mine, still wrapped around my arm.*

*"Duncan, that's us."*

*I couldn't take my eyes off the kids. The bloody scene continued to unfold but I couldn't bring my eyes to it. I didn't need to.*

*I remembered.*
*I remembered everything.*

# Chapter 30

Duncan

*The sickening recollection flooded the empty corners of my mind. This was all my fault. How could I have let that happen to her. It was me he was after. Not her. She paid the price for my resistance. For my weakness.*

*The cost of my disobedience was a life.*

*He was right – I wasn't worthy of love.*

Heidi

Duncan and I both startled awake.

What. The. Fuck.

I clicked on the light that sat atop the bedside table. Duncan was sitting, with his head resting in his palms. I placed my hand on his back and rubbed his hardened muscles. "Duncan, are you okay?" He sat quietly for a while before my phone rang, distracting me. The screen flashed with Graham's name. I answered.

"Hello?"

"Heidi. How is he?"

I looked over at him, assessing the state he was in. His knees were brought up, close to his body, his elbows resting on top of his knees.

"No wonder he couldn't remember. He suffers from dissociative amnesia. Maybe this was a bad idea."

I couldn't form the words, but I had to agree. "I think I need to call you back."

"Okay. But I'm here if either of you need me. Honest. If Duncan needs support, I'm here."

"I appreciate that," my words fell flat. I did appreciate his offer, but holy fucking shit. I didn't know if Duncan would recover from this. Again.

"Reach out if you need me."

"Okay." It was barely a whisper. The line disconnected and I turned to face Duncan again.

He was still. So still. I wanted to touch him but was afraid.

None of us anticipated to see what we saw. And even more, I hadn't expected to be hit with the realization that I had witnessed that once before. I had known this part of his past before I ever knew his present. But like Duncan, I forgot.

As a child, I always had the most vivid dreams. Each one feeling like a memory. One night in particular, I remember seeing a little boy, he looked to have been my age, bawled up in the corner of an empty room. When I approached him, he said he was scared and needed help. At the time, I didn't understand what he was asking. We were sitting in an empty room. What could he possibly need help from? But, as time passed, my dreams would progress with more details, eventually depicting the same horrific scene we relived tonight.

I remembered any time I dreamt of the boy, he was always adamant that he wasn't worthy of love. But even then, I knew that wasn't true. I even told him as much. *Well, you're my friend and I love all my friends. And that means that I love you!*

As I sat, pieces that I didn't even think were from the same puzzle started to fit into place. Those dreams weren't mine like I thought. Instead, they were Duncan's and I had unknowingly Connected with him when we were barely six years old. The realization sank deep into my soul. My heart twisted with regret that I hadn't remembered sooner. If I had, maybe I could have saved him from this pain. Instead, I walked him right into it.

And while we successfully figured out how my house dream tied Duncan and I together, we hadn't figured out how Tawny tied into all of this. I filed the thought away for another day.

I reached my arm out to touch Duncan's arm. "Duncan –" He recoiled immediately.

"Heidi, don't."

His tone was cold. Almost as cold as the man dressed in black. "But I need you to know that –"

He practically jumped out of the bed, away from me. "I mean it, Heidi," he snarled.

His heavy footsteps paced around his room. All I could do was watch as emotion wracked his body. Anger, sadness, regret, fear, cowardice. His fists tightened by his sides, causing the veins in his arms to raise. His shoulders were tensed. His brow furrowed above eyes that shot daggers to anything his sights laid on. Which eventually landed on the dresser.

With a quick force, he bent and snatched my duffle bag from the floor of his closet before storming over to his dresser. The drawers where I had just packed my clothes away before bed were now being snatched out and emptied.

Fear and heartache built in my throat, "Duncan, I

don't understand."

"You can't be here." He couldn't even look at me. "I'm sorry."

"What is there for *you* to be sorry for?" My question fell on deaf ears as he shoved my clothes into my bag before making his way to the bathroom and bringing my toiletries.

"Please. You don't want to do this. I know you don't."

Silence.

"I love you, Duncan. Please!"

"You shouldn't." He zipped up my bag and left the bedroom. I remained still, wrapped in his sheets, until he returned. "You should go."

*No no no no no no.*

"Where do you want me to go?"

"Anywhere but here. I'm sure Graham would welcome you with open arms."

*Oh.* I scoffed. No way could he mean that. If his words didn't betray him, the way his body flinched at his own words did. Still, he wouldn't bring those enchanting green eyes of his to meet mine. "And what about our baby?"

"He'll be better off without me too."

*Nope. Fuck this.*

"Duncan Johnson, have you lost your damn mind!" I was fucking livid. I rose to my knees and perched on the edge of the mattress as I shot fire from my eyes at him. "Look at me!"

He refused.

"I'm sorry that I forgot too. I'm sorry that I walked you back into that horrifying memory. But you said no more running. You promised!" Tears burned my cheeks as they fell aggressively from my eyes. I was standing now, crowding him. His arms crossed firmly across his bare chest as he looked over his shoulder, still refusing to look at me. "This doesn't define you." I didn't let his lack of acknowledgment stop me. "I said look at me. Look at me and tell me why you're walking away. Again. Tell me why you're breaking your promise. Tell me why I'm not good enough for you to keep. To keep *us*." My voice cracked, hoarse from the tears and emotion scratching my throat. When he didn't look at me, I placed my hands on his abs, gently dragging my fingers down almost reaching the waist band of his sweatpants. "Fine." My voice was a cracked whisper. "You want me to go? You'd rather Graham takes care of what's yours?"

I felt his body stiffen and I had hoped it would have been enough to get him to crack. But it wasn't. If I had to play dirty to knock some sense into him, I would.

I slid my fingers thought the soft trail of body hair that led to his cock. "You'd rather it be Graham that I touch like this?" I slowly dropped to my knees in front of him, dragging my hands down the tops of his thighs, sure this would break him. "You'd rather me be on my knees... for Graham?" He jerked his head and trained his gaze on me. His mouth formed a straight line and his arms remained folded across his body. His chest rose and fell with each agitated breath. His cock also rose, pressing against the soft fabric of his pants. He wasn't responding to me, but his body certainly was.

The last time he was swallowed by silence and

grief, after his dad's diagnosis, this was how he recovered from the upsetting news. By our bodies just reacting to each other, allowing euphoria to roll through us, flooding his mind with enough oxytocin to push him away from the darkness. He said he needed to feel safe and that's how he felt with me. I knew in my gut that hadn't changed.

It wasn't the time, or the place, but if he didn't get his shit together quick, I'd snatch these sweatpants down, exposing his length and wrap my lips around him. Let him think about me doing the same to Graham.

My hands danced up and down his thighs, moving closer to his erection, begging him to break his silence and answer me. When he didn't, my lips curved into a wicked grin as I staired up at him. I tucked my fingers into the waist of his sweatpants and started to tug them down.

Green eyes flashed with desire before fear set back in. I licked my lips, ready to fully expose his length when he snatched me up by my arms, causing me to release the top of his pants. "You can't do this, Heidi. You can't be here."

"Why!" I cried out. Frustrated that my plan hadn't gone according to plan. "Tell me!"

"Because –" The loud boom of his voice shocked both of us and regret flashed across his face. "I couldn't protect her."

"Duncan, you were six! How could you?"

He shook his head and took a seat on the edge of his bed. "You don't understand. I could have prevented it. He asked me to go with him and I said no."

Duncan's head dropped, as if the weight of the truth was hung around his neck. I knelt in front of him, sitting back on my heels to ask, "Who is he?"

"That was my dad."

I trapped my gasp between my lips. The revelation lingered between us as we both processed it.

"And he killed my mom." He winced with despair, and I nearly lost it. I shot up to my knees and wrapped my arms around his middle, squeezing him tightly, as if I was trying to wring the anguish out of him. His hands finally wrapped around me as he buried his face into my neck and shoulder. I could feel his damp face against my skin.

We stayed like that for a few minutes, just breathing each other in, grounding ourselves in the present. Once he sat up straight, releasing me from his arms, I stood and used the hem of my shirt to dry his damp checks. Hope filled my chest when I was rewarded with a small smile.

"Duncan, you know that none of that was your fault, right? You can't carry that around with you anymore."

He shook his head. "If I would have gone with him, we would have left, and she'd still be alive." He rested his face in the heels of his hands and wiped away the emotion from his eyes. "Heidi, how am I supposed to continue living life knowing that I took one? How am I supposed to expect you to love me after this? That monster's blood runs through my veins." His eyes shot to my stomach, reaching out to rub it gently. I knew where he was going with this, and I refused to let him torture himself any further.

"I need you to hear me when I say this, because I will not be repeating myself." I rested my arms on his shoulders and zeroed in on his eyes, trying to hold in my tears. "You could *never* be capable of committing such a disgusting act and neither could this baby. You are not responsible for what happened. And I couldn't image any parent not wanting their child to live a fulfilling and happy life after such a tragedy. You've suffered enough. And to answer your second question, there is nothing, absolutely nothing, that you could do to make me stop loving you. I am yours, Duncan. Always."

He sat, staring at me for what seemed like minutes, his gaze flicking between each of my eyes. Despondency replaced his irises and I almost thought I had lost him. But when he heaved a heavy sigh, relief washed over me.

"Tell me what happened. Let me help you carry it."

Duncan hesitated, but eventually he shared every detail that had been hidden in his mind all these years. He explained that he didn't get to see his dad often because they moved around a lot. And that night, Duncan wasn't even supposed to be at the house. His mom had left him with the neighboor while she was at work. "I had forgotten something at home and wanted it. Our houses were right next to each other. I didn't think there'd be any harm in running across the yard to grab it. But when I got inside, he was there too. We never locked our door, so I didn't think anything about it. I was actually excited to see him. But he became agitated when I refused to go with him. He told me I wasn't being a good son. That good sons didn't disobey their fathers. My mom showed up a little while later and they got into a fight." He blew out a forceful breath, calming his emotion. "All I did was ball up in a corner and cry. The entire time my mom was forced to fight for her life, I did nothing. Once he was done, he looked at me with such hate. So much disgust. And that's when he said, 'Ain't no son of mine gonna cry like a little bitch.' Then he spit at me when he said, 'You're not worthy of my love'. Then he turned around and left me alone with my mom's bloodied, lifeless body."

# Chapter 31

## Heidi

Duncan had eventually fallen back asleep. After baring his soul, he laid his head in my lap and I rubbed his head and shoulders, doing my best to bring any type of calm to him. I rested my head against the headboard and my thoughts ran rapid in my mind.

I hated that he would have to process this all over again. I wanted to help him through this because he deserved to be happy. He deserved to live a life full of joy and love without having to answer for someone else's egregious crime. But at the end of the day, in the bottom of my gut, I knew it'd be his decision. It would all be up to him if he wanted to carry that weight or not. There would be no amount of love that I could show him to change that. Not even this baby would be enough to save him if he didn't want to be saved.

Eric taught me that. He was loved so deeply by his ex and his daughter, but it didn't stop him from taking a drink. It didn't cure him. The same would be true for Duncan. I could love him and support him for the rest of my life, but healing would be completely up to him.

Finally, the thought I had put off for last. Before Duncan fell asleep, he so casually, through a drowsy haze said, "I need to find my sister."

He had a sister.

My mind raced with worry. If he had a sister, why

wasn't she with him when at the orphanage? Or if she was, did she get adopted by another family? The questions spun like a web in my mind, each one creating a new thread.

The sun had been up for well over an hour when Duncan finally stirred awake. I dragged my hand through his hair, "Good morning."

He stretched his arm up and behind his body as he twisted before settling back into his same spot. He wrapped his arm tighter around my thighs and snuggled in closer to me. He lifted his head and eyed my belly, then me. He pressed his lips against my stomach and left them there. I thought I had felt his body shudder, but I couldn't be sure. When he pulled away, he pushed himself up to a seated position and faced me. "I owe you an apology."

"No, you don't." He didn't. Everyone processed trauma differently.

"Yes, I do." He pulled my hands into his. "It's not an excuse, but I'm still learning how to handle... all of this. I can't seem to get my shit together, and each time, you take the brunt of it. This is what I worried about. I had always told myself that I needed to deal with my past before I could truly settle down. I knew this would be a disaster and at this point, I'm scared that you'll resent me. Not that I could blame you for it."

"Oh," I climbed on top of his lap and wrapped my arms around his neck. "I don't resent you. I don't think I could. I just want you to know that I will be here for you..." He sensed my hesitation, and it broke my heart further. "But it will be up to you if you truly want to heal. There's not enough support that I could offer you to force you to work through this. This will be a decision that you have to make on your own."

He nodded swiftly before kissing me deeply, his large hands braced the back of my head and back. His love poured out through his kiss, making it difficult not to melt against him. He pulled his lips away and pressed his forehead to mine. "Please, don't give up on me."

"I could never."

***

"Hey." I said to Olivia as I busted through the door of the store. "Thank you so much for covering for me." I shot past her, not registering if she heard me or not. I threw my stuff on the desk in the office before turning on my heels to head back to the counter. "It's been a night. I don't even know –" I noticed Olivia staring at me wide eyed. "What?"

Her eyes flicked to the wall with the coolers. I followed her gaze. Esther Shaw was pulling a carton of eggs from the cooler. She was an eavesdropping, gossip spreading nana. She was the one who told my mom about Duncan meeting a woman in Easton City all those weeks ago. Not that we were together then, but she liked to put her nose where it didn't belong.

She must have felt Olivia and I looking at her. She turned around and addressed me. "Oh, Heidi. How are you dear?" Like she didn't hear the bell ring as I blew through the threshold.

Yeah, I'm not falling for your innocent granny act. "I'm great, Ms. Shaw. How are you?"

"I'm good, dear." She approached the counter and

loaded her basket on top to the counter. "Olivia, dear. How are you and Ronny? Has a date been set for the wedding yet?"

Olivia, the poster child of well-mannered daughters, smiled brightly and scanned her items. "Not yet. But I'll be sure to let you know as soon as we decide."

Esther smiled and handed me her basket once it was empty. "Heidi, correct me if I'm wrong. But did I see you and Duncan leaving together the other night?"

I surprised an eye roll. I thought quickly about how to answer her question. I didn't want to be too forthcoming, but I also didn't want to lie because she'd be able to tell. Ultimately, I settled on the truth, there was no need in continuing to hide it. "You did."

"I see." She eyed me curiously, waiting for me to elaborate.

But I didn't. It wasn't her business. I guess I would have to see what the rumour mill came up with next.

She paid her total, took her groceries and left.

"You enjoyed making her sweat," Olivia said.

"Well, she's a nosy nelly and I wasn't going to give her the satisfaction. And to be completely honest, I can't believe Mom hasn't shouted it from the roof tops already."

"I guess there's still time," Olivia joked.

I took a seat next to her behind the counter, crossed my arms over top of the counter and laid my head down. It wasn't even eleven o' clock yet and I was exhausted.

"What happened." Olivia asked.

I groaned in response. "I don't even know where to start." I sat up again but slouched. "But it's really Duncan's story to tell so I should probably let him be the one to tell it."

She nodded understandingly. "Well, how are you feeling?"

"Overall, I'm okay. The nausea comes and goes and I'm a little tired but I'm alright."

"Good. How'd it go with the parents?"

"Surprisingly, it went well." Olivia's eyebrows raised with shock. "I know. I thought I'd get at least one tongue lashing. But nope, she said she was incredibly happy for us."

Olivia laughed. "Maybe you've worn her down."

"Ha! Wouldn't that be something."

"When is your next appointment?"

"In about three more weeks. They'll be once a month for a while. But enough about me. Have you and Ronny really not set a date yet?"

"Not yet, we're waiting for me to find a dress. Which leads me to my next question… Will you come with me tomorrow to go dress shopping?"

"Yes, of course!" I squealed. "This is so exciting!"

"I'm sorry it's so last minute. I know you've had a lot going on."

Guilt wrenched my gut. I'd been so caught up in my own drama that I hadn't paid much attention to her. "I'm so sorry. I've been a pretty shitty sister."

The bell above the door rang, stealing both Olivia and I's attention. Mom walked in with a cooler. "Hi girls."

Someone was in a good mood. "Hey, Mom." We

said at the same time.

"I thought I'd pop over and bring you girls some lunch. Hope you're hungry." She sat the cooler down on the counter in front of us. As if her placing the lunch box down was a queue for my stomach to growl. "Oh, Heidi," she tsked, "you're carrying a baby. You shouldn't let yourself get hungry. You should always keep a few healthy snacks on you." She busied herself with placing the food in front of us. "I brought you a couple of different things – I wasn't sure what you might be craving." A bowl of broccoli cheddar soup, a chicken salad sandwich, a small bowl of fruit, and a peanut butter and honey sandwich all sat in front of me. She then sat a single sandwich in front of Olivia.

Well, this was new. Mom hasn't catered to me like this since I was a kid. I eyed her suspiciously. "Mom, you feeling okay?"

"Yes. Of course. Are you?"

I eyed Olivia and she just shrugged her shoulders. "Okay, what's the deal? Why are you suddenly so understanding and…and nice?"

She zipped up the lunchbox and pushed it towards Oivia, silently asking her to put it behind the counter. "I just want to make sure you're doing okay."

Words unsaid hung in the air between us. "But…"

She fiddled with a napkin she brought and held her gaze towards it. "Not a 'but'. An 'and'."

"Okay…and…"

"Esther called me…"

I suppressed an eye roll. Esther moves fast.

"She said you seemed to be stressed –"

"Mom, Every –"

"Let me finish." Her eyes finally caught mine. "She called to tell me you seemed to be stressed when she was in here earlier. And well... well I told her to mind her damn business."

Olivia and I were both shocked, our jaws hung. "Why would you do that, Mom?" Normally my mom would gladly listen to the gossip that rolled through these boring streets.

"You've got enough going on right now. You don't need a bored nana making things worse for you."

"Oh. Well, I really appreciate that, Mom. Thank you."

She reached across the counter and patted me on my arm. "Of course, sweetheart."

I tried to let the moment pass peacefully but I couldn't stop the nagging question from burning the tip of my tongue. "I'm sorry. I just... that can't be all. Right?" I looked between Olivia and my mom, making sure I wasn't the only crazy one here. "I mean, you've been fairly calm about the recent curveballs in my life and that's not like you at all. So please, if this is just an act, I'd rather know now so I'm not blindsided later."

My mom sighed and started fiddling with the napkin again, "All I want, for the both of you, is to be happy. And you, Heidi my dear, have been absolutely miserable since your senior year of high school. And don't think I didn't notice that you also stopped hanging out with Duncan around that same time. I don't know what happened, but I tried not to pry. Hoping the two of you would work it out, or come to me or Annette for advice, but neither of you did.

After that, I tried anything and everything to get the two of you back together." She offered me the kindest smile I've seen on her in a while. "Honey, the two of you belong together. I can't explain it, but it's always been so obvious. And everyone deserves to be loved the way Duncan loves you."

I didn't know if it was from the pregnancy hormones or if I actually believed her, but I started to sniffle back my tears. I hopped off my bar stool and rounded the corner to give her a hug. And not just an obligatory hug, an actual hug. She squeezed me tightly to her and my tears flowed unapologetically. I felt Oliva join us and the three of us stood there, crying and hugging then eventually laughing. It was like with each tear shed, all the bitterness that built up over the past ten years washed away.

Using the napkin she clutched in her hand, she dried the tears from Olivia and I's cheeks before cradling my face with her hands, "Can you forgive your ol' stubborn mama?"

I coughed out a joyful sob, "Only if you can forgive me too."

Once Mom left, I told Olivia that I'd cover for her if she wanted to take the rest of the afternoon off. She'd been holding down the store a lot lately. Thankfully she agreed and left a few hours after Mom did.

The rest of the day was incredibly slow, but it gave me time to follow up on a nagging suspicion. I text Graham to fill him in, because once again, I needed his help.

# Chapter 32

## Duncan

"So, your mom gave Esther the business, huh?"

"She sure did," Heidi said with a giggle. "She told her to mind her *damn* business. I still can't believe it. I'm only sorry that I couldn't see the look on her face as Mom said that."

"Yeah, it would have been amusing, that's for sure." I reached across the middle of the truck seat and rested my hand on her knee. "I'm glad you and your mom are moving towards a better relationship."

She turned and leaned her head against the headrest and beamed at me as she said, "Me too. It feels like I can breathe again. Even all the tension I usually carry around in my shoulders has disappeared."

"Good." I said with a smile as I continued to stroke her knee with my thumb as I drove down the highway.

We were headed back to the city. Olivia and Heidi were going dress shopping and Ronny and I planned to check out a couple of suits. While we were here, we would also have to stop by the institute.

After I acted like a complete fucking fool the night before last, and after Heidi went to work, I visited my parents. I told them everything. Not just about the details that I remembered from my childhood, but also how I acted towards Heidi.

"I'm not going to pretend to know what you're

going through," my mom had said, "but the child therapist you used to see said that survivors of trauma usually blame themselves. But make no mistake, son, what happened is not your fault. Your birth mother protected you because she loved you. That's what mother's do. We protect our children. We do it without hesitation or regret."

All those years I had tried to fill in the gaps of my memory, I made assumptions about my past and why I was no longer with my birthparents. None were ever remotely close to the truth. Like Heidi, I woke up feeling a little bit lighter this morning now that I had finally remembered, but a different type of heaviness settled in my chest.

I eyed the box in the floorboard by Heidi's feet. The few items it contained could have only been put there by one person. *My sister*.

If she was still out there, I needed to find her. My parents said they were unaware that I even had a sibling, that no one at the orphanage told them about her. I couldn't remember her name though. It was on the tip of my tongue, but I couldn't grasp it.

I needed to find her.

\*\*\*

It took Heidi and Olivia much longer to pick out a dress than it took Ronny and I to pick out our suits. We were able to get fitted for our suits and eat our entire lunch before they called us letting us know they were done. They seemed happy when we arrived back at the bridal shop and Ronny asked, "So?"

"It'll be ready in two weeks!" Olivia whooped,

the glow of saying 'yes' to her dress still radiating from her grin.

Ronny wrapped her in his arms and spun her around as he kissed her. He pulled out his cell and scrolled through the calendar app. He and Olivia pointed to the screen counting over the weeks before nodding in agreement. "It's settled then. In just three short weeks, September twenty-fifth," he beamed and wrapped his arm around her, pulling her in closer. "The day I get to call you my wife." Olivia planted a brief kiss on his lips through a muffled squeal before turning to Heidi, releasing her full excitement.

Heidi squealed, matching her sister's enthusiasm. With both girls squealing like they were, I worried onlookers would think something was wrong, but no one even batted an eye. In the midst of their fit of excitement, Ronny explained that Olivia had her heart set on a specific dress but didn't know how long it'd take to come in or how long alterations would take. Now that they knew, they wanted to get married as soon as possible.

Once the girls finally settled, we said our goodbyes and Heidi and I headed to the institute.

"You ready?" Heidi asked as we parked in the parking lot of the institute.

I sighed, letting a few responses pass through my brain before settling on one that wasn't snarky or ungrateful sounding towards Graham for offering his help. "I'm as ready as I'll ever be." And that was the truth. I've gone through therapy before, but I wasn't too keen on the idea of Graham being my therapist. "Didn't you say he was hiring a new doctor?"

Her hand was already on the door handle when

she turned back to me. "Yeah. He said they're in their final round of interviews and should have a candidate selected next week."

I nodded. If I could hold out for a week, I could see the new doctor instead. Heidi was right, it was up to me to want to heal from this. With her support and therapy, I knew I'd be on the other side in no time.

We exited the truck, and I rounded the back, meeting her at the tailgate as she handed me the box of mementos. She felt it was important to bring it today. I wasn't sure why, but I didn't question her.

The receptionist nodded towards us as we entered, and Heidi nodded back. Heidi then led me back to a room that I hadn't been in before. It was plush and bright inside. The indigo color of the couch was an odd choice if you'd ask me, but it looked soft and comfortable.

"You can go ahead and have a seat. I'm going to let Graham know you're here." I walked further into the calming space and took a seat on the couch. I was right, it was comfortable. "And if you need me, I'll be right across the hall in the empty office. And remember, you can leave at any time."

The way she said the last part made me nervous. "Leave?"

She nodded, "Yes. You don't have to stay if you don't want."

"O-kay."

"K. And remember, I love you."

Was she nervous about how I was feeling about Graham stepping in as my active therapist? "Don't worry, babe. Everything will be fine. I'll be on my best behavior." I rose to my feet and walked to the door where she continued to stand and landed a swift kiss on her lips. "I love you too."

She offered me a half smile and shut the door behind her.

A moment later I had returned to my seat and a quick knock landed on the door before Graham stepped inside and took a seat in the chair across from me. Regardless of how helpful he was being, the sight of him irked me.

"Duncan," he offered a curt nod.

"Graham," I mimicked. I could see the smart ass comment he was prepared to make dissipate. Guess he was heading Heidi's request too. Playing nice and taking the high road.

"How are you feeling?"

"All things considering, I'm fine."

"Great. I'd like to introduce you to someone, but I want to make sure you're mentally feeling sound."

I thought on his question for a moment? Was I mentally sound? I thought so. "I'm good." Whatever I needed to do, whoever I needed to meet, as long as it was a step closer to being whole for Heidi, I'd do it. Hopefully it was the new doctor they were considering hiring.

He nodded, "Excuse me a moment." He peaked his head out the door briefly, before stepping to the side and gesturing with his arm towards the second empty chair next to his.

A blonde woman entered and took the seat Graham offered. I didn't recognize her until she lifted her head to face me. She was the same woman Heidi was speaking to the other day when we were here.

"Duncan, this is Tawny."

Tawny? The name pulled a thread deep in my mind. The woman's eyes were glassy and damp. *Well, I guess she's not the new doctor like I had hoped.*

Graham spoke again, "Duncan, if you feel comfortable, could you please show Tawny the items in your box?"

Looking between Graham and this woman, I could sense the importance of his request. Reluctantly, I pulled back the flaps and pulled out the first item – the toy figurine.

Her hands flew to her mouth as she gasped.

As she did, the mental thread that was previously tugged on had completely unravelled now. My sister's name was Tanya, but I called her *Tawny*. "Tanya?" I asked, wide-eyed, my chest weighed heavy with disbelief.

She nodded profusely as her eyes squeezed shut, forcing tears to fall from her eyes.

Graham slowly back out into the hallway. "I'm going to give you two some space." He shut the door, leaving me with my sister.

"How are you here? Why are you here?" My questions sounded accusatory, but I was genuinely curious. How was it that she was here, literally right here when I only just remembered her a day ago? Her tears were coming hard and fast. I noticed the box of tissues on the table beside me and handed them to her.

She pulled a few before blowing her nose in them. I waited for the sobs that wracked her body to subside. "Where do I begin?"

"From the beginning."

She blew out a breath and started from the top. She first explained how she came to be a patient of the institute.

When I was here, meeting with Kathrine to negotiate the bid last month, she said she saw me. She didn't know who I was, of course, or at least hadn't been certain. She said my eyes were what she recognized, not the man behind them. They looked exactly like our mom's.

A small smile peaked at the corner of my mouth, I remembered. She had beautiful eyes, and I was lucky to have them too. I asked why she wasn't at the orphanage with me. It was the only thing I didn't understand.

"I lived with my grandparents – my dad's parents. They were too afraid to take you in too. They assumed your dad was the one who was responsible and feared he'd come after them next. We had hoped you'd be able to tell police what you saw but you didn't. Or couldn't. That's when I grabbed your things." She nodded towards the box. "I wanted you to have a few things from home so you wouldn't be scared. They sent you to the furthest possible orphanage to keep you safe. But after that, they kept transferring you across state lines and I lost track of where you went. The last orphanage I found that had any recollection of you was over in Mallard Bay. I moved here to Easton City in hopes that you weren't far."

"How long have you lived here?"

"About twelve years."

A devastating realization sank in. For twelve years my sister lived two hours from me and didn't even remember her.

"I never stopped looking for you. That's why I go by Tawny instead of Tanya." Tawny looked off to the side a little like she was watching an imaginary scene play out in front of her. "You never could quite say Tanya right, it always came out as Tawny. Whenever I'd ask around for you, I'd always say Tawny, in case you came looking for me too."

"I'm sorry that I forgot about you. I didn't mean to. I –" Tears welled up in my eyes. I pinched them away with my fingers. "I only just remembered recently."

"Oh, Duncan, you don't have to apologize. *I'm* sorry I couldn't find you sooner. "I appreciate you saying that." I took a few tissues and had to wipe my own eyes. Once I felt my voice wouldn't crack, I asked, "Did they arrest him?"

"Who? Mom's killer?"

"Yes. My dad."

She shook her head. 'No. There were no witnesses besides you and there was no evidence to tie him to it. Everyone assumed it was him, but they couldn't make anything stick. I also think he was the one responsible for attacking me earlier that same day. I think he found me and followed me home." She paused to dab the corner of her eyes with a fresh tissue. "We moved around so much after you were born. He wouldn't leave Mom alone and at the time, no one wanted to make enemies with him."

"Why?" I remembered us moving a lot, but I didn't know why. Maybe I was too young to understand.

"Because he's Rhett Miner, son of Robert Miner,

the most ruthless leader of the Kansa City Dusk Prowlers. Any enemy of Rhett's is an enemy of Robert's, and no one wanted that over their head. No one wanted to make a blind accusation against either of them."

"I'm sorry, what's a Dusk Prowler?"

"It's a motorcycle gang. And from what I hear, they're still very much active."

"Wait. Let me get this straight. You're telling me that our mother's murderer is still out there, possibly terrorizing more people?"

Tawny frowned and nodded her head.

"Then we need to stop him."

# Chapter 33

## Duncan

My knuckles rapped quickly on the door to the empty office before pushing it open further. Heidi shot from her seat with a hopeful look on her face. "How'd it go?"

I rushed towards her and swept her off her feet, planting an appreciative kiss on her lips. "I don't know how you did it, but I know this was your doing. I will forever be grateful to you."

Her grin widened, "So, it's her?"

"It's her, babe."

Heidi expelled a breath of relief. "I'm so sorry I couldn't tell you. Patient confidentiality and all."

"I understand." I rubbed my hands from her shoulders, down to her wrists. "But, can I ask you for a favor?"

"Of course. Anything."

"He's still out there. Tawny said he was never arrested."

"I know," her eyes full of sadness. "I'll help you find him, Duncan. But, first let me make a call." She pulled out her phone and scrolled through her contacts before pressing send. After a short moment, she finally said, "Detective Reid, It's Heidi Miller. Do you have a moment?"

\*\*\*

I spent the next couple of hours talking with Tawny while we waited for Detective Reid to arrive at the institute. She had led a relatively normal life after she was adopted by her grandparents. She, like me, also went through intensive therapy after what happened to our mom. She didn't witness it, but she saw the scene once the corner removed our mom's body.

That's when she found me, still balled up in the corner of the kitchen, sitting in front of a puddle of blood. She said she had to push herself past the police barricade to get to me. She was eleven when it all happened.

She also explained a little about her life before me. Our mom and her dad married right out of college. However, when she was two, her dad passed away from a car accident. Tawny said she wasn't sure how our mom and my dad met. Tawny hadn't known she was dating anyone.

"But I remember when mom explained that I was going to get a little sister or littler brother, I was beyond excited. I had hoped for a sister so we could play dollies together," she chuckled, "but you turned out to be a great little brother. You would follow me around everywhere. And while you never played dollies with me, you would bring your Action Man to rescue them if they were hurt."

I eyed the box that held those once forgotten objects and smiled. That Action Man was a toy I got out of a cereal box. I thought I was the coolest kid in school because my cereal had toys inside. Tawny had made sure it went with me when Child Protective Services picked me up.

My eyes burned from the memory. A strange woman, prying me from my sister's arms before setting me in the backseat of a car. Blue and red lights poured in through the windows. Blood was crusted in my hair, the side of my face, my hands, and body. That's how close I was, or that's how angry he was, as blood flung from his knuckles with each pull of his fist.

"Duncan, it's not your fault." She read my mind. "I could just as easily blame myself because I'm the one he found. He followed *me* home." She leaned forward, resting her elbows on her knees and pulled on a serious expression. "We did not do this to our mom. There is only one person responsible and it's not either of us."

Heidi said it. My brother and parents have said it. Hell, even Graham has said it, but I didn't believe it until I heard it from Tawny – *It isn't my fault*. It's not hers. It's his – my biological father – he's the one responsible. But I'd do everything in my power to make sure he was held accountable for what he had done.

A knock on the door interrupted us and Graham popped his head in. "Reid's here. Heidi's in there speaking to him now."

Tawny and I filed into the hallway and followed Graham into the nearly empty office that once belonged to Dr. Keller.

Detective Reid wasted no time as we entered the office. "Mr. Johnson, Miss Miller here says you have a crime to report."

"Yes, sir. I'd like to report the murder of our mother. It happened in Kansas City nearly twenty years ago and my biological father is the one responsible."

"Kansas City? What's your father's name?"

"Rhett Miner."

Reid's mouth agape, "Miner? There wouldn't be any relation to a Robert Miner would there?"

"One in the same," Tawny spoke up.

"And you are?" Reid eyed her curiously.

"I'm Tanya or 'Tawny' Fletcher. Our mother," her thumb flicked between the two of us, "Janet Fletcher was murdered."

Reid continued to eye her suspiciously. "Uh huh. Any witnesses?"

"Yeah. Him."

Everyone's eyes landed on me.

"Is that true?" Reid asked.

I nodded, "Yes. I was there."

Reid eyed Heidi before bringing me back under his grumpy and suspicious eye. "Then why didn't you report it back then. Why wait till now?"

"Because I lost my memory from that time. I only remembered recently."

Reid furred his brow even further as he pinched his nose, "Listen –"

Graham interjected, "I'll be happy to explain the science behind it if you need, but dissociative amnesia is a real diagnosis. It's incredibly common for survivors of trauma to experience it, especially in children."

My eyebrow quirked towards Graham, curious as to why he was defending me.

Reid let out a gruff sigh, rested his hands on his narrow hips beneath his round middle, "Fine. I will look into it. I'll see how far my reach is. Kansas City is halfway across the country, but I'll see what I can do."

"Thank you, Detective Reid."

He grumbled something and gave a pointed look to Heidi before exiting the office. Heidi followed behind him.

I noticed Graham's gaze following Heidi before it landed on me. "Hey, man. I appreciate what you did for me back there."

"No need. A murderer is still out there and deserves to be brought to justice. It's obvious that Reid is still having a hard time coming to terms with our abilities." He started to head towards the door but stopped short and turned towards Tawny and I. "I truly am sorry about what happened to your mom. It's not an easy fact to accept when one parent is responsible for taking the life of the other."

His words were genuine, I realized. He had suffered a similar tragedy. *Did Graham and I have something in common?*

"So, what do we do now?" Tawny asked from beside me.

"We fight like hell to bring Rhett to justice."

# Chapter 34

## Heidi

Today was the day!

I stood behind my sister as she stood in front of the mirror, giving herself one final look. She pushed a curled tendril over her shoulder to join the rest of the curled strands, blanked by an elbow length veil. The beaded sweetheart neckline of her laced boddice sparkled from the afternoon rays seeping in through the windows. The lace continued down the skirt of her gown, ending in a short train. I smiled, gently squeezing her hand with excitement. Our matching Bride and Maid of Honor bracelets adorned our wrists.

We heard the door open behind us as Mom and Dad stepped inside. From the reflection in the mirror, we watched as a mix of emotions flashed across Dad's face. "Honey," he held his arms out as he approached her, "you look stunning." Tears welled in his eyes as Olivia turned and embraced him.

"Thank you, Dad." She fanned her face once he stood back, admiring the both of us.

"Look at my girls," He gestured to Olivia, then to me. "You're getting married, and you're having a baby." His voice cracked slightly from the emotion threatening his words, "Where did the time go?" Mom walked up, and rubbed her hands against his shoulders and she hugged him from behind. "It seems like only yesterday the two of you were out in the yard, kicking up my freshly raked pile of leaves to make leaf angels."

We chuckled at the memory. It would take Dad forever to get them all piled up, and no sooner could he open a bag to rake them into, Olivia and I were falling backwards into them, sweeping our arms and legs out wide.

He placed one hand on each of our shoulders as Olivia and I stood side by side. "I am so proud of the women you both have become."

"Aw, Daaaad." Oivia and I chorused as we fanned or eyes rapidly.

"Okay, no more making us cry," Mom swatted the air with her hands, shooing Dad from us. "It took some of us hours to look like this. Not all of us have the luxury of rolling out of bed looking as handsome as you."

Dad smiled coyly and jokingly puffed up his chest, "You think I'm handsome?" He playfully wiggled his eyebrows at her.

"Oh, Arnold," she chortled as he planted a sweet kiss on her cheek. She finally turned to Olivia and held her hands. "Are you ready?"

Olivia nodded, sniffling back tears of joy. "I've been ready."

Mom turned to me and gently squeezed my elbow, "Come on, let's get you lined up."

I turned and gave Olivia a quick kiss on the cheek. She and dad linked arms and assumed the position. I followed Mom to the back door of Ronny, and now also Olivia's house.

"Wait till you hear the song change, count to three then come on out," she said, giving my arms a reassuring squeeze. She exited and a moment later, I heard the pluck and singing of violins from the music outside.

*One. Two. Three.*

I opened the back door and made my way to the white carpeted path and started making my way towards the alter. The vibrant orange and yellows from my sunflower and gladiolus bouquet paired beautifully with the cream-coloured chiffon of my dress. It was a beautiful contrast between subtle but bright.

I was busy focusing on my steps, making sure I wouldn't trip over the long skirt, when I felt the burn of his green gaze. My eyes fluttered to him, drinking in his tall statue. The silhouette of him in his suit, the way it fit snug around his broad back and thick thighs made his hard body look even more defined. Reflexively, my tongue darted over my lips in response.

How was it that the man could make my mouth go dry but the spot between my thighs wet at the same time. The blush was rising to my cheeks. I had to look away before I turned beat red. The way he looked lovingly, but hungry at me made me swoon and sweat.

I took my place on the opposite side of the alter of Ronny and Duncan. The speakers that were set up in the middle of the yard started playing the sounds of church organs, singling that the bride was on her way.

The whole town came out to witness these two get married today. The chairs that sat on either side of the aisle, all aligned in neat lines and rows were all mix matched. Everyone brought their own chairs instead of us borrowing them from the lodges around town. It was true Mount Hopewell fashion.

Dad and Olivia appeared in everyone's view and the crowd stood as we watched her make her way down the aisle. I peeked over at Ronny. His eyes were watering up at the sight of his soon to be bride making her way toward him. Duncan gave Ronny a supportive slap on the shoulder that said, 'I'm happy for you'.

Olivia and Dad hugged before she handed me her bouquet and joined hands with Ronny.

Tim, my parents' best friend and our Mailman cleared his throat, opened his black binder and began to read from the pages. "We are gathered here today…"

\*\*\*

The cake had been cut, the bouquet and garter had been tossed and the sun had set over an hour ago. The chill was starting to settle around us, but no one seemed to mind it. Likely due to the warmth from the alcohol buzzing through them. Everyone, except me had a drink in their hand. A detail it seemed that Esther had also noticed.

Now that I was twelve weeks pregnant, I felt we were in the clear to tell people that Duncan and I were expecting. However, with Olivia and Ronny's wedding the same week, I decided to wait until after they said, 'I do'.

I walked inside the house to grab a few more meatballs and to steal a few minutes of warmth. As I leaned against the counter, enjoying both the warmth and nourishment, I thought about Detective Reid. I pulled my cell from the dress pocket concealed by too many layers of chiffon and thought about texting him.

Asking Reid for his help with locating Rhett came with a condition. Graham had to partner with third-party sleep specialists and psychologists to have all the science behind Connecting peer reviewed. My job would be to provide proof that Connecting was legitimate and to submit for any additional electroencephalogram scans that may be required throughout the review. This process would be necessary in strengthening the case against Graham's mom, Dr. Jamie Keller.

Graham had already shared all the data with the specialists required by Detective Reid, and they were only just getting started on their peer review. Who knew when they'd be finished.

*My* only condition to Reid's condition, however, was that I got to help find Rhett if their efforts didn't turn up any leads.

Neither Duncan nor Graham was okay with my part in either condition. They worried it'd be too much stress on the baby. Luckily for them, we lived in a civilized society, and I was not being locked down in a basement somewhere while evil scientists conducted experiments on me. And as far as locating Rhett was concerned, I promised to *only* get involved if the police needed help locating him. If it came down to that, and I found a way to successfully Connect with him, I would only observe and not interact. The goal would be to blend in with the rest of his dream until we could locate him physically.

But it's been nearly three weeks since Detective

Reid agreed to help us locate Rhett, and I hadn't heard an update yet. I was becoming antsy.

Roars from the reception outside grew loud as Duncan quickly stepped inside before shutting the door behind him, quieting the celebration and the cold. "There you are."

"Yep. I Needed a snack and some warmth." I slid my phone back into my pocked and plucked another mini meatball from my plate with a toothpick before popping it in my mouth and chewing it up. "They're so good. Want one?" I plucked a new meatball and held it towards him.

He smiled and shook his head. "I just wanted to come check on you." He crossed the kitchen, removing the meatball from my grasp and setting it back down on the plate. He wrapped his arms around me, warming me with the heat of his body. I melted against him and allowed him to hold my body weight as I went limp in his arms. "Esther is out there asking everyone if they've noticed that you haven't taken a drink all night."

"Yeah," I chuckled against his chest. "I've noticed her noticing my lack of participation."

His hands grazed down the length of my hair, "Are you still planning on making the announcement tomorrow?"

"Honestly, I'm a little curious to see how long it'd take everyone to notice," I joked. His chest bounced with a snicker. "Yeah. I'm still thinking tomorrow." I tilted my head back to look up at him, resting my chin on his chest. "What do you think?"

"I think whenever you're ready to tell people, I'm ready." He leaned down and kissed my forehead,

"I'm following your lead, babe."

I felt a yawn coming on, and I buried my face in his chest to try and suppress it, but it was no use.

"Ready to get out of here?" he asked. I nodded, my head still resting against his chest. He ran his strong hands down my arms, to my hands, steadying me. "I'll go get the car warmed up and be right back." He gave each hand a gentle squeeze as he backed away before turning to head through the house to the front door.

The side of my thigh vibrated, and I retrieved my phone from my pocket. The screen lit up with Detective Reid's name, I answered immediately. "Hello?"

"It's Reid. We found him."

# Chapter 35

## Heidi

The following morning, Mom decided she wanted to come keep me company at the store while Olivia was off. She'd be off today and the next few days, enjoying her honeymoon. Not surprising, neither she nor Ronny wanted to go anywhere to celebrate it. They just asked that no one disturbed them while they were "busy".

If it were me, I didn't think I would be able to pass up the opportunity to visit someplace new. Even though my desire to travel hadn't been as important as it once was, my desperation to leave these mountain roads behind me for a while nearly vanished. However, I knew I'd regret it if I didn't.

Since I started working at the institute, I'd been more than fulfilled. I realized only recently that I didn't seek adventure from travel like I assumed, but adventure from new experiences in life.

Experiences like having a meaningful job. Helping my patients in their journey of healing had been beyond rewarding.

When I met Eric, he was nearly broken, barely being held together by the love he had for his daughter. Now, he was progressing well through therapy. He hadn't needed me to intervene during any of his Connections this past week. Under the instruction of Graham and I, he would put himself in a compromising position, usually at a bar, and could successfully and effectively refuse all alcohol offered to him. Graham also mentioned that Eric's moods had been balanced and positive lately too. Eric was starting to believe that this time his sobriety would stick. Knowing that he would eventually be able to rebuild his relationship with his daughter made my heart swell with pride and awe.

Also, and I would never tell my mom this, but being in a relationship was an experience on its own. One I happily enjoyed. Duncan and I had been officially living together for the past three weeks and I'd been deliriously happy.

Not that any relationship defined me, but it was something I had wanted since I was seventeen. Waking up next to him each morning, wrapped in his brawny embrace was not something I thought I'd ever be fortunate enough to have. Navigating our lives as a couple, integrating our lives together, preparing to be a family for our child, were all bonus that broke up the dullness of our lives before.

My phone buzzed under the counter. Picking it up I saw it was a message from Duncan.

**Duncan:** Just saw your mom, she asked me to tell you she'd be there in just a few minutes. Also, I'm leaving for the city now to file the police report with Graham. Reid asked for a statement from him confirming my diagnosis too for "credibility" purposes. Said it'll help push the process along to get an arrest warrant. I love you. I'll call you when I arrive.
**Me:** Okay, drive safe. And I love you too!

Much to my surprise, Duncan and Graham seemed to come to some sort of understanding. Not a friendly one, but one of mutual respect. Graham hadn't been forward or disrespectful of Duncan and I's relationship since the day he found out I was pregnant. I was grateful. They had finally pulled their heads out of their asses, and I no longer had to referee them. But their occasional glares at each other didn't go unnoticed.

Some of the tension was relieved once Graham finally hired a new doctor to replace his mom at the institute. Duncan, knowing that going through therapy again would bring up raw emotions, didn't want Graham overly familiar with him and his demons. It was true, they now shared a common demon, but it didn't mean they'd be wearing BFF necklaces any time soon.

The bell above the door rang as Mom pushed the door open, an insulated bag hung by a strap over her shoulder. "Sorry! I'm running behind this morning." She sat the bag down on the counter in front of me. "Did Duncan let you know I would be here soon?"

"Yes. But why are you in such a hurry?"

She was already busy unpacking the insulated bag and the aroma of my current craving hit my nose, singling the loud rumble from my stomach. "Well, I wanted to make you breakfast before heading over. I had pancakes and bacon cooked up and plated and was just about to head out the door when Duncan arrived. He mentioned that you'd been eating this for a week straight." She unwrapped the strawberry cream cheese, egg, and sausage English muffin breakfast sandwich and slid it over to me.

Unsuccessfully, I attempted to blink away the tears that formed in my eyes.

"Honey, what's wrong?" Her expression shifting to sudden worry. "Is that not what you wanted? I can make you something else if you'd like."

I shook my head as I wiped my eyes and cheeks with my hands. "No. I just – I just." I sniffled and tried to dry more tears that fell. It seemed silly, but this simple gesture made me feel so loved.

Duncan, so aware of my cravings, was able to tell my mom about them. Then my mom remade my breakfast for me just so my craving would be fulfilled. The warmth that spread across my chest was almost too much to handle. "Just, thank you, is all. I really appreciate it, Mom."

Her features softened and she came around the counter to dry the rest of my tears with the napkin she pulled from the lunchbox. "Of course, sweetheart." She planted a quick kiss on the top of my head before pulling her own breakfast from the bag and taking a seat in the rocking chair. "Now eat up. Gotta keep your body nourished to keep that baby healthy." There's the Mom I knew. I laughed, then took a bite of the delicious display of affection.

Finishing up the last bite of my sandwich, Tim entered the store, greeting both Mom and I with his toothy wide grin and a nod. "Good morning, ladies."

"Morning, Mr. Tim." I wiped my mouth with a napkin and stood from the bar stool. "We don't usually see you in here on Sundays. To what do we owe the pleasure?" My mom had yet to greet him, I noticed. She remained suspiciously quiet from her rocking chair.

"Well, I hear a congratulations in order."

*Ah. Now I get it.* I chuckled at my mom's eagerness to tell everyone about the baby. And for some reason, I wasn't bothered by it. "Yes, thank you." I intentionally eyed my mom, hoping she could feel my gaze tickling the side of her face. It worked.

She hopped up from her chair with excitement, "I'm sorry! I just couldn't keep it inside anymore. You said you wanted to wait until after the wedding." She held her hands up, palms facing out, "And, in my defence, I did wait until the end of the night. Besides, Tim is family."

"It's okay, Mom." I meant it. I turned back to Tim, offering a friendly smile, "Duncan and I are very excited."

"Good." He patted his hand on the counter with a grin. "I was wondering when you kids were going to find your way back to each other."

I still didn't understand how it seemed that most everyone knew about the feelings that Duncan and I shared. As teens, we thought we were careful, keeping our affections private. As an adult, I spent so many years trying to push my feelings down, ignoring them so I could forget them and move on.

Gravel crunched outside, signalling someone pulling into the parking lot. Then another. And another. I turned to face my mom again. "Mom, how many people did you tell?" She stared, her expression giving her away, she'd been caught red handed. "Mom?" I asked expectantly.

"Everyone!" she admitted, gleefully and apologetically. "I told everyone…"

Tim laughed and all I could do was shake my

head, unsurprised and amused. "Might as well meet them outside. No need in everyone cramming inside." Tim reached the door and held it opened for Mom and me as we walked outside.

I couldn't get fully out of the door before everyone yelled "Congratulations!" Mr. Ed, Mrs. Margie, and Mrs. Trudy all exclaimed as they approached the front of the store to crowd me with hugs. In the corner of my eye, I saw Esther Shaw, eyeing me with disappointment.

"Oh, Esther," my mom hollered towards her. "Wipe that look off your face."

"Well, why am I always the last to know stuff around here!"

"Because you're always the first to put your nose in other people's business," Mrs. Margie replied.

It sounded rude to me, but the four women laughed and Mrs. Esther made her way to us. "I'm truly happy for the two of you."

\*\*\*

Duncan was home by the time I pulled into the driveway and parked next to his truck. I couldn't wait to tell him how he missed the congratulations tour from everyone and that my mom actually spilled the beans to everyone last night.

It felt good, everyone knowing. For the first time in a long time, I was thankful that this was my home. These people were my community, my family. I was fortunate to be able to raise my own family here.

Climbing the stairs to the front door, to the house we shared together, my heart was exceptionally full. I wasn't sure how much more love I could absorb before melting into a puddle of tears.

Opening the door to greet Duncan, I became breathless at the sight in front of me. Orange gladiolus pedals were scattered all over the floor of the living room. Candles were lit and strategically placed around the room. In the middle of the floor stood Duncan, wearing his usual style of a black tee shirt, a pair of medium wash denim jeans, and his dusty brown work boots. He was the epitome of ruggedly handsome with his short, tousled hair, full beard, and thick muscles.

I entered further into the space and shut the door behind me, tears already welling in my eyes. Duncan's grin reached his alluring green eyes, making me swoon. He held out his hand for me to join him. I shed my purse and sweater on the floor where I stood and took his hand.

He pulled me in close to him, cupping the side of my face as he leaned in and kissed me deeply. Our lips released and his hands found mine and his eyes met my tearful expression.

"Heidi, our love has always felt stronger than a basic mix of emotions. Our love is more of a tethering, a binding, that connects our souls. You have been the force driving me forward in life, providing strength and safety, even when I wasn't aware. There are not enough minutes in our lifetime to describe all the ways you amaze me, and even less to list the reasons why I don't deserve you."

Duncan released my hands to reach into his front pocket and retrieved a little black velvet box. He lowered himself onto one knee and opened it. Inside sat a stunning oval cut, moss agate engagement ring with a rose gold band. Simple yet spectacular. My hands flew to my mouth in surprise. The damn had broken, releasing more tears.

"Heidi Miller, will you allow me to love, support, and protect you for the rest of our lives?"

With my hands still covering my mouth and tears spilling down my face, I nodded enthusiastically. He rose, lifting me up as he did, and spun us around, my arms wrapped around his neck. Finding his lips with mine, I pressed too many kisses there before trailing them all over his handsome face. "Yes, Duncan, yes!"

I slid down the front of his body and planted my feet in front of him. He plucked the ring from the box before sliding it onto my finger. I looked sanguinely at my finger, admiring my first and most special piece of jewlery, and our life together flashed before my eyes.

And oh, how beautiful it was.

# Epilogue

Three Years Later

Duncan

Staring at the people gathered around us today, a sense of belonging filled my chest. These people welcomed me into their town with open arms, without knowledge of who I really was, what I had endured, or who I would become.

Every heartache I had experienced in my life, I was sure, led me to this moment right now. My eyes immediately found her, a true vision in the white satin that graced her curves. Her long wavy brunette hair flew behind her as a breeze rolled across the lawn of our yard. I couldn't help the smile that grew across my face, the emotion that filled my eyes, as I watched her walk down the aisle towards me.

"Mommy pretty, daddy."

Towards *us*.

Our son, Walker, carried the name my birth mother gave me and her eyes. I scooped him up in my arms and held him on my hip as Heidi got closer. Her hazel eyes brightened at the sight of us, her infectious smile causing our son to giggle with a sweet laugh.

As soon as she was close, Walker practically leaped from my arms to her. Clinging to his mom he squeezed her tight. "So pretty, mommy." A chorus of "aww" sang at the sweet display.

Heidi's hand rubbed his back tenderly, "Thank you, buddy." She pressed a kiss on his cheek. "Want to sit with Grammy and Gramps or stand with me and daddy?"

"Sit." The crowd laughed at the toddler's response. Arnold, held out his arms for Walker, kissed Heidi on the forehead then took his seat with the rest of our family.

I held out my hand for Heidi to join me. She accepted and stood in front of me. My heart pounded behind my chest, counting down every second before I could seal our commitment with a kiss.

I was completely lost in the hazel mistiness of her eyes when I heard her finally say, "I do." I didn't wait for Tim to announce us as husband and wife. One hand cupped the side of her face, the other pulled her closer. I dipped down, finding my *wife's* lips with my own, surrendering, completely incurable of her.

***

Heidi

There was no mistaking it, Duncan and I were bound together beyond words and emotions. I was living my dreams.

The love,

The family.

The passion and excitement of life.

Everything I had once dreamed and hoped for was in front of me.

Duncan and I turned, we raised our arms in celebration as everyone stood and cheered. I found our parents, all four of them puffy eyed from emotion. Olivia and Ronny clapped and whooped for us. Walker and his cousin Alice sat on a blanket on the ground in front of them. Both grinning and clapping, mimicking the adults around them. Next to Oliva sat a teary-eyed Tawny.

She eventually bought Olivia's house once it was listed for sale. Her and Duncan had grown close, and if you didn't know any better, you'd never know they went nearly twenty years without each other. Tawny was a welcomed addition to the Sibling Supper we hosted every other week. The Johnsons had also included her as one of their own. She would often visit with Gerald, during his chemo sessions.

Then, a few rows further back sat Graham. My friend. The one who helped me along this path to uncover my ability. The one who understood the joy and burden of what we were both capable of. As time allowed, he and Duncan were able to get over their macho bullshit. They weren't overly friendly, but the past was in the past, and they dared not to bring it with them to the future.

These past three years had been a whirlwind. Duncan, Graham, and I were all required to testify in both Dr. Jamie Keller, and Rhett Miner's murder trials.

Dr. Keller's charges were ultimately upgraded to murder since her husband, Martin, ultimately died. She was sentenced to twenty-five years to life.

Duncan had to submit to a DNA test to prove he was in fact the son of Rhett Miner. Duncan's testimony of what he witnessed that terrible night was the nail in Rhett's life sentence.

Connection Theory had also been peer reviewed and confirmed. More psychologists were participating in dream therapy and building the science whenever new discoveries were made.

Still, with the therapy being more popular, no one else had yet to show promising scans that would indicate they had the ability to Connect.

My eyes flashed to my son's precious face as he rushed towards Duncan and me.

"Up daddy." His arms were stretched upwards as he perched on his toes in front of Duncan. Duncan bent, lifting him up and holding him so he could look out at the guests too.

Duncan hooked his arm out for me, "Well, my wife, shall we?"

"Yeah, mommy, cake now?"

They way Duncan's face lit up when he called me his wife, and the way my son's matching green eyes lit with excitement for cake both amused me and melted my heart. "Yes and yes."

As we followed the path away from our friends and family, towards the cake our son had his eyes, and stomach, set on, I took in an appreciative breath. My world had finally found harmony and awareness.

My dreams, which once caused so much uncertainty and confusion, now brought me clarity. As it turned out, they were more than a series of meaningless images that danced around my mind.

# Acknowledgments

As always, a special thanks to my circle of support. Without y'all, I may not have had the courage to do this. Thank you for always listening to my ramblings about my plots and characters.

To my readers, THANK YOU for reading In His Dreams. I hope you enjoyed it as much as I enjoyed writing it. I wouldn't be able to continue to follow my dream without your support.

This story was important for me to tell because we live in a world where it's often looked down upon to struggle with inner demons. We don't all come from solid families to help us process the troubles we face. Sometimes, our families are the cause of it.
Either way, you're not alone.
You are brave.
You are worthy.

With love and appreciation,
Olivia Pelar

# What'd ya think?

Reviews go a long way, especially for independent authors like myself. Any rating, any words, are always appreciated it. If you're inclined to do so, you can leave your review on Amazon, Goodreads, or the retailer you purchased the book from.

You can also follow my Amazon Author Page for updates on new releases.

# About the Author

Olivia Pelar is an indie romance author. Her love for creative writing, good mysteries, and steamy romantic stories has inspired her to leave it all on the page. When she isn't working on her next project, she's spending time with her family, snacking, and reading through her ever-growing TBR.

Connect with me on Instagram @
Instagram.com/Oliviapelar.author

www.ingramcontent.com/pod-product-compliance
Lightning Source LLC
Chambersburg PA
CBHW070057260626
47160CB00004B/1236